NETAGIRI

Also by the same author

The Average Indian Male
Karl, Aaj aur Kal

NETAGIRI

CYRUS BROACHA

EBURY PRESS

An imprint of Penguin Random House

EBURY PRESS

USA | Canada | UK | Ireland | Australia
New Zealand | India | South Africa | China | Singapore

Ebury Press is part of the Penguin Random House group of companies whose addresses can be found at global.penguinrandomhouse.com

Published by Penguin Random House India Pvt. Ltd
4th Floor, Capital Tower 1, MG Road,
Gurugram 122 002, Haryana, India

Penguin Random House India

Published by Random House India in 2014

10 9 8 7 6 5 4 3 2

ISBN 9788184004915

Typeset in Sabon by R. Ajith Kumar

Printed at Repro India Limited

www.penguin.co.in

FSC www.fsc.org MIX Paper from responsible sources FSC® C047271

This is a legitimate digitally printed version of the book and therefore might not have certain extra finishing on the cover.

To my son Mikhaail,
my daughter Maya,
and my German Shepherd Ruffo.

You guys often wonder why your dad doesn't have a job. I could take the easy way out and say I'm not your dad. Instead, I've decided to write a book. After reading this book you'll know why I don't have a job and why all three of you must work very hard to provide for me. Especially you, Ruffo.

Your…er…dad.

Author's Note

The only way to explain this story is with one word. It is the same word that has been used by critics to describe Billy's *Hamlet* and Homie's *Illiad*. The word is 'incomplete'. It is now both a literary and scientific fact that all great works are bound together by that one very same quality: they are all incomplete. This is why we invite you, our friendly reader (especially those who've been administered all their shots), to complete this tale. In order to facilitate your cooperation, we have kept plenty of space available for you to fill up on every page. Also, in case you are troubled greatly by the book, the publishers are open to the idea of sharing the author's entire medieval history with you. But they warn me to warn you that his medieval history is both longer and funnier than this book.

Introduction

After his first book, which was semi-autobiographical, and then a second, which was as close to a foray in socio-cultural anthropology as a weightlifter could make, with this third book *Netagiri*, Cyrus Broacha surely enters a thoroughfare that was earlier traversed only by the likes of Henry David Thoreau, Aldous Huxley, and Lalu Prasad Yadav. Politics.

Ordinarily, politics is not a subject you would bargain for Cyrus Broacha to commonly attempt. The topics you'd expect him to write about would be 'The Cryological Genesis of the Hair Weave', 'The Entomological Nature of the Common Tick', 'Metaphysical Poets from Cusrow Baug', and 'How to Measure the Bust of a Female Bodybuilder'. So you'd probably think of this book as a departure.

But politics to Cyrus is second nature. Not many people know that he established himself as a seasoned political practitioner from the day he first pinched his Montessori teacher's behind and blamed it on Pakistan. He's never looked back since.

As a young boy studying in college, he never once bought a textbook, pen, or paper but instead borrowed from any poor willing soul; all the while insisting he try out a socioeconomic system structured upon common ownership. He called it Communism.

As a sophomore actor on the English stage, he celebrated many an opening night—drinking with the cast at popular drinking holes, enjoying the social brotherhood that theatre inspired, never having to reach into his wallet. To him this was co-operative management of the economy. He called it Socialism.

As an anchor on television, he acknowledged and welcomed all suggestions, opinions, and directives, encouraging every single person to participate in the decision-making personally. He then proceeded to do exactly what he wanted. This was his version of Democracy.

Today, as a married man with two young children, he honestly believes he is living in a Dictatorship.

With such practiced political beliefs, Cyrus could have easily found vocation as chief political advisor to Muammar al-Gaddafi or Pervez Musharraf but chose to pursue a less dignified life in satire.

Having been intimately involved in his career as a satirist for the last, give and take, twenty-five years and, especially in the last eight as partner in the weekly political send-up television show, 'The Week That Wasn't', I have faithfully watched his growth as he turned from amateur to professional and from ectomorph to endomorph.

His intuition, understanding, and perspicacity in grasping political rumblings and nuances is exceptional. His ability to spin a solemn story into a whimsical yarn and ruthlessly witty satires is unparalleled. And with his ever-questioning intelligence, he possesses the best perspective to take on this dubious subject, Politics.

I imagine *Netagiri* will be uproariously, hilariously, side-splittingly funny, and an exciting and priceless read for you. I will tell you for sure if I decide to read it.

Kunal Vijayakar

Introduction to Introduction

This is a huge mistake folks. Firstly, a work of fiction doesn't ever have an Introduction. For this I blame the publisher who believe this to be a true story. However, this is as big a yarn as man descending from apes is.

Secondly, I have never met this person Kunal Vijayakar and I deny all accusations of proximity between himself and me quite vehemently. Furthermore, his usage of words such as 'Sophomore actor' 'Cryological Genesis', and 'Socialism' are absolutely wrong as none of these words exist in the English language. His facts are all over the place. I never ever pinched my Montessori teacher's behind. I merely pressed it gently for 14 minutes. Twice. I also didn't blame it on Pakistan.

Lastly, I deny being married, although I may have discovered two children. I ask you, dear reader, to disregard the paranoid rantings of this delusional delinquent Kunal Vijayakar forthwith. I ask you instead to pay far closer attention to the paranoid rantings of this delusional delinquent namely myself instead.

Prologue

Long, long ago...or was it last month? No, long, long ago...actually some time ago...er...look, stop pressurizing me. I don't have all the details, but what I have, I'll share with you.

Although time is not clear, the geography certainly is. Our tale is set in a country which is on the right of Australia, just below North America, and very close to present day East Timor (or was it on the right of North America?). Look, the best I can do on such short notice is that the country was next to Nepal. It was a largish country and had all the features countries should have—mountains, rivers, two wild animals, traffic jams, incomplete road construction, bridges with no utilitarian value, dengue, dust, dirt, and a politician every square mile. Oh, and a partridge in a pear tree.

It was an impressive enough country. Especially if you'd never been there. It was called 'GYAANDOSTAAN'.

This roughly translates into 'a place of two pieces of knowledge'. And it was a crime to spell the country name in small letters. You had to use capitals. GYAANDOSTAAN. Even if you were just thinking of the name in your head. The Gyaandostaanis (citizens) spoke their own language. This was mistakenly called Gyaandostaani. In fact, the Gyaandostaanis didn't speak Gyaandostaani. They spoke Pupric. Gyaandostaani was spoken by a few tribes that lived off the eastern side of the Russian Steppes. Now Pupric is a very difficult language. It has no consonants. Only vowels. As a result, it appears to the outside ear as a collection of wailing sounds similar to the plaintiff cry of lost Emperor Penguins. Since you, dear reader, are not familiar with the plaintiff cry of Emperor Penguins, I have translated everything from the original Pupric into rudimentary English which can be understood by 5-year-olds who incidentally are my main reading market. But to simplify things and not make a hillside out of an ant hill, let's call the language Gyaandostaani anyway.

GYAANDOSTAAN'S capital was a city called Bey. Both the action, and the lack of action (depending on how you rate this book at the end of it), takes place in Bey. Now, since this book will never release in GYAANDOSTAAN—well, it may not release in Nepal either—I've decided to use capitals for GYAANDOSTAAN only when I feel it necessary. And I will feel it necessary when I need to fill in the page with bigger letters for the noble purpose of finishing off the story as quickly as possible in order to avoid being sued by the Emperor Penguins mentioned at the beginning of the story. Story being the original idea, but we may diversify into ditty, poem, love lyric, or even leaflet, depending of course on market conditions.

A brief history of Gyaandostaan would be warranted here. But, I don't want to be accused of spoiling you, dear reader. As the great Freddie Mercury once allegedly told his accountant, 'Too much detail can kill you'.

Our story, in short, traces the rise of a young politician, who could have easily been mistaken for Napoleon if he was one inch taller. He rises to power with Napoleonic speed and takes the country to dizzying heights.

This book is all set to be a motion picture. And the list of actors who have turned down the lead role include Nasseruddin Shah, Irrfan Khan, and possibly, Darsheel Zaffary.

GYAANDOSTAAN'S climb is a lesson to the whole

world that you can go far in life, even if your country has a strange name.

Although the story's beginning is a straight lift from Herman Melville's *Moby-Dick* (original version), the rest of the story is almost original, and the music is perchance, never lifted. Our tale starts where most books ought to start at, a funeral.

In sector 36 of mid-town Bey, in a palace about twice the size of Buckingham, and with no Welsh corgis, the grand patriarch of the Huskee clan, Jay Huskee, had just passed away. To tell you the truth, he had passed out of a balcony window after losing his balance. He fell into an open truck carrying seaweed to Oceania. Within minutes, he was deep at sea, never to be seen again. His family took out a search party to sea, to see, but abandoned the mission after nine minutes, primarily because it started to drizzle, though of course not precisely where they were, but about 15 miles to the Northwest.

Grandfather Huskee was a career politician. Nobody knew his real age because he hadn't told the truth in 38 years.

Our story now starts with the family having returned home after the customary last rites. Since Jay Huskee's body was never found, this was performed with his favourite lighter and a handful of seaweed (perhaps, his last known adversary).

Our tale opens on the first dinner after this monumental event. (Keep in mind GYAANDOSTAANI tradition requires four days' mourning followed by three days' recovery before dinner can actually be served. If it is served before this, it must be served only on one leg.)

1

It was a big, old house (which I suppose is different from an old, big house, although I have no idea why), especially by Gyaandostaan's standards. Bear in mind, houses were not owned in GYAANDOSTAAN, they were 'occupied'. All you had to do was enter an abode and never leave, which may or may not explain why the rock group The Eagles wrote 'Hotel California' after a weekend in Bey.

By GYAANDOSTAANI standards (not the language that is spoken in Gyaandostaan, but the place), it was huge. Bey was a thinning town where most people happily lived like cockroaches. A 400-square-feet one-bedroom house easily contained an average of eight to ten residents. In contrast, the Huskee's place was a seven-room, five-bathroom mansion, with a swimming pool and a terrace garden. In keeping with the philosophy of dumping down their wealth, the

Huskee's swimming pool had no water, and the terrace garden had only two plants, both made of ceramic, which Mrs Huskee (Jay's daughter-in-law) insisted on watering twice a day. Now that you mentioned Mrs Huskee, let me tell you a little about her.

Sophia Huskee was born probably many years ago. She worked in a law firm where she met Y. Suresh Huskee, Jay's son. Since she was pretty and he influential, they quickly pretended to fall in love, and soon got married. Jay's wife had died when Y. Suresh was just 5, so the early marriage was welcomed by the Huskee clan. Jay's wife was actually a very nice lady, except for the fact that she had a man's first name—Mohan—which was a continued source of embarrassment to Jay. Invitations would say Mohan and Jay, which made the duo sound like out-of-work music composers. As Jay earned fame and power as a politician, his wife's first name came even more into prominence. So when she died suddenly of an illness which I cannot pronounce properly, he quickly looked on the bright side, and oh yes, immediately started answering all invitations.

Sophia and Y. Suresh produced two sons. Well, technically Sophia produced and Y. Suresh may have contributed. The elder one was called Paul. Paul was in fact an original Pupric name. Meticulously it was spelt and pronounced exactly the same as the Christian version, Paul. But I assure you there was no relation between the two Pauls. The second son was named Mohan after his grandmother as a tribute to her.

Paul and Mohan were pleasant enough boys. Mohan was perhaps a bit too pleasant. And as he grew up, his fondness for the opposite gender became less and less apparent. Paul was an avid sportsman and soon became obsessed with Gyaandostaan's national game of darts. He became the school captain, the envy of all. However his 'darts' career ended when, during a state tournament, representing Bey, he pierced the forehead of a rival school's principal standing seven-and-a-half feet from the dart board on the other side of the road.

Paul was a popular boy in school and college, and had, at an early stage, decided he wanted to be a leader of men. An incident told by a school friend, Vandy, confirms this. 'Paul was once dropped from the handball team by the school captain. Paul first thought he'd practice hard and get back into the team. It then dawned on him to do the right thing, which he did. He complained to his grandfather. Within 48 hours the team captain was removed from the school itself. Paul was made the skipper of the handball team, Emeritus for Life. Handball in GYAANDOSTAAN was a very different sort of a sport. Basically you could touch the ball with any body part, save the hand. Or the other hand. Thus it was very close to football, which is very close to soccer. However, there is no word for soccer in Pupric, so it was conveniently called handball. And now, I beg you please don't ask me what football was called!

However, it was around this time that another incident occurred with the Huskee family.

Y. Suresh had, for the past year, started going for advanced yoga classes. His teacher was a svelte, sexy, young yogini called Shanti. Shanti was so good that she could take on three yogic positions, simultaneously. She was arguably on the list of 'Sexiest Women of All Time' along with Marilyn Monroe, Halle Berry, and that hot chick from your class whose name I now forget. The family should have figured something was wrong when the half-hour session started stretching to five-and-a-half hours. They should have at least started having doubts when the class's location changed from home to the Imperial hotel, room 609. And they really should have had second thoughts when the class started lasting a full three-day weekend.

One fine day, Y. Suresh, not cut out for politics, not having worked a day in his life (which actually meant he was cut out for politics), did the famous Gyaandostaan rope trick. You know the one where the rope disappears? He and his positions manager just clean vanished.

Of course nobody really missed him. And Jay immediately started grooming Sophia as the next in line for power. As for the boys, the only effect it had on them was that Paul distanced himself from yoga forever, and that Mohan gave up wearing spandex for a month.

It's important to set up the Huskee family here, because the actual story will take up only four printed pages. So we need to discuss something else for a while, and I feel football has been done to death, quite frankly. So let us return to the first dinner, after the sad demise of the venerable old statesman—Jay Huskee.

Our story opens in the long dining room of the Huskee residence where Sophia Huskee is sitting disconsolate, upset, and depressed, as she can't find the orange sari belonging to the duly departed patriarch. In keeping with her depression, she's wearing a parrot green shiny chiffon 'paanglu'. A 'paanglu' is exactly the same as the Indian salwar-kameez, though strangely there is absolutely no connection between the two cultures, Gyaandostaan, being a far more ancient and complexed culture as evidenced by the fact that no Gyaandostaani spit in public.

The fact that the patriarch liked to dress in sarees (albeit in private) was something that Sophia never brought up in front of the family. Not out of any perceived embarrassment or affront, nor because she was petrified that once out in the open, Jay Huskee would start wearing all her clothes. The real reason was that she had taken a fancy to one of his orange sarees.

For ten minutes at the dinner table, no one spoke. Then Sophia decided to help everyone come to terms with their grief. This she did by dividing his personal things among those present.

Paul immediately looked at his grandfather's grand room, as well as his collection of shoes (his grandfather owned over 200 pairs of shoes; some were even of the right size). Mohan was given the rest of his belongings. Inwardly Sophia hoped he wouldn't get the orange saree. At this point the door burst opened and Mr D'Souza entered.

People who thought nicely of Mr D'Souza would have compared him perhaps to a Russell's Viper. In reality he was even more peculiar. He wore white pants, a white shirt, gold-rimmed spectacles and had slicked-back hair. His hair was jet black, which was not common in a 60-year-old in Gyaandostaan. Mr D'Souza dressed the same all year round, whether it was for office, a family picnic, or a cocktail party. He was very close to Jay Huskee, some said *too* close. In fact, the day Jay fell out of the window, Mr D'Souza was standing next to him. This set tongues wagging. However, it didn't make sense for D'Souza to rid himself of his mentor. As Huskee's principal secretary, he enjoyed all the trappings of power only as long as Jay Huskee was around. His explanation was that he tried to hold on to Huskee, but got an almighty sneeze at the same time. And as his hands flew to secure his nose, Jay Huskee flew out of the window.

It was Mr D'Souza who saw him fall into the truck and bounce thrice up and down. And it was D'Souza who noted down the truck's number and colour, information that he gave to the police (red truck, no. 78113) later. And although both facts turned out to be absolutely wrong (it was in fact a green truck, no. 4914), every little piece of information always helps in ultimately putting together an entire jigsaw puzzle. Mr D'Souza and Jay Huskee had been together for 30 years and although Sophia had never seen them actually do more than hold hands, she had her suspicions, having occasionally seen Mr D'Souza in a blue chiffon 'Paanglu'.

For now though, everything remained cordial. D'Souza was urged to join the dinner table, which he did by holding on to the centre portion extremely tightly. After a few bites of the 2-week-old potato salad, he started to speak.

Now D'Souza mumbled and spoke very quickly. Generally, he was far less audible than Marlon Brando as Marc Anthony. Hell, he was less audible than Marlon Brando chewing paan and talking as Marc Anthony under water. In fact he was less audible than the actual Mark Anthony playing Marlon Brando!

Mr D'Souza: 'In these matters you need a warning.' (In truth, he said 'Sector 36 is in mourning'.)

Sophia exerted him to eat more of last month's salad. D'Souza continued now with the extra challenge of three medium-sized potatoes filling his cheeks.

Mr D'Souza: 'He's become really tall.' (Actually it was 'The people want Paul'.)

He went on to elaborate his point for the next half hour. Since his point wasn't audible, the whole exercise took one and a half hours. For Sophia the good news was that he consumed, on his own, the entire contents of last year's potato salad, and though she wondered why he hadn't choked on it, she was pretty confident the best was still to come.

D'Souza's discourse ran very clear. Apparently in the GYAANDOSTAAN constitution, on page 78 (right after the article on dog's poop being the sole responsibility of the dog and his owner, in that order), it was mentioned that if a member of parliament died an unnatural death, whilst still in power, then a family member would take his place, even if the family member had never actually won or even fought an election.

As Mohan was too young, and more importantly wore mascara, D'Souza felt Paul would be the obvious choice. Of course there was the obvious fear—falling out of an open balcony and disappearing into a handful of seaweed may not be considered completely unnatural. However, D'Souza felt he could cross that tributary only at the right time. He asked the family to think about this, as the wounds were still fresh. Sophia responded by dragging out some even older potato salad which she packed into a doggy bag for the ol' faithful to take home.

As he exited the room, Sophia could have sworn she saw some orange material caught in the zip of his briefcase. Could it be? No way. Could it be that the famous highly coveted, orange saree was with Mr D'Souza? This threw up a whole heap of unanswered questions.

How did he get the orange saree? Did Jay Huskee and him share the orange saree? Was there a second orange saree? Was Jay wearing the saree when he flew out of the window?

And did D'Souza know that Jay Huskee knew that she knew about Jay Huskee's saree, and also knew that she knew that he knew she knew? And that she pretended not to know that she knew, he knew, she knew?

As the door shut on the man in white, Sophia returned to the dinner table. She seemed greatly relieved. Not because D'Souza had left, but because she had finally successfully offloaded that awful salad. Soon, the family resumed what appeared to be a normal dinner experience at the Huskees. This could be gathered from the simple fact that no family member said a word to another. Mr D'Souza's words reverberated in their ears. As usual no one was completely sure what those words were. But for the sake of expediting the process, we must all take it as pushing Paul's name forward.

2

A large collection of phenyl, uric acid, and decomposed liquid fertizers divided the city of Bey into two halves. Of course this was initially a river, but now its deep purple chemical colour meant if you washed your face in it, you lost your eyebrows. The upper side was where the rich lived and the poor worked. The lower side was where the poor lived and the rich made the poor work, more.

The Huskee patriarch's office was located here downtown. It was a three-storey building called Daffodils. In Gyaandostaan, it was customary for every major city to have at least one building called Daffodils in it. Three decades back, it was the name Sunflower which ruled the roost. Of course before that it was the era of Petunia, which itself rose from the glory days of Rose.

Paul sat patiently in the main chamber, listening

patiently to Mr D'Souza's offerings. Patience being the key word because, as I said earlier, with D'Souza you had to listen to what he said, and then decipher the words correctly—a two-pronged process which always led to prolonged time consumption in even simple dialogues.

D'Souza's very opening remark caused a ten minute to and fro, tête-à-tête. Paul clearly heard 'hey', but it actually was 'they'. However D'Souza couldn't complete his sentence because Paul kept replying to the greeting. The opening remarks went from Paul's point of view:

D'Souza: 'Hey...'

PAUL: 'Hey.'

D'Souza: 'Hey...'

PAUL: 'Hey.'

D'Souza: 'Hey…'

PAUL: 'Hey.'

Now to open your eyes, dear reader, and to show a balanced, healthy, and unbiased view point, let's examine the same dialogue from D'Souza's viewpoint.

D'Souza: 'They...'

PAUL: 'Hey.'

D'Souza: 'They...'

PAUL: 'Hey.'

D'Souza: 'They...'

You can see that D'Souza was not popular on the cocktail circuit and phone calls were simply unbearable. Once again we need to fast forward to a point where this conversation takes a turn for...well...let's just leave it at, takes a turn.

PAUL: 'Hey.'

D'Souza: 'They...let me complete Paul.'

Paul: 'Did you say "what strong forearms, doll"?'

As the hours passed, in order to stop himself from choking D'Souza to death, Paul insisted they turn to the computer and take a more 21st century approach to chatting. So they sat back to back and continued the introductions on their respective computers.

Since the whole 'chat' took over two hours, and I know you dear reader cannot absorb any chat that goes over one and a half hour, I shall condense it into one paragraph which may or may not be on this page.

Essentially, D'Souza exhorted Paul to take over his uncle's political position as the Honourable Minister of Parliament and preside over all his charities and humanitarian efforts, which would all come to naught if the MP position was not occupied by a family member quickly. The list of charities included a printing press, a rubber factory, two high-rise commercial buildings, a fleet of high-end private taxis, tuition classes, an engineering college, a waste management factory, and the one NGO his grandfather was most passionate about and proud of—an air conditioner manufacturing business with the famous tag line, 'You're never too old to be cold—HARPOON Air conditioners'!

After the verbal tennis marathon passed, D'Souza brought in the crack team that Paul had inherited from his grandfather. These would be the sultans that would support his political career as well as execute far more important functions like carry his bags, point him in the right direction, help him avoid being hit by a bus, teach him to floss and gargle simultaneously in an effort to save time, and help him garner a large bank of excuses, the fundamental unit on which a lasting political career is made.

Now before we go further, please understand, again, the names we are about to reveal (yes, I 'm not writing this account alone; for God's sake there are thousands of contributers) may sound fiendishly similar to sub-continental names. However, this is just a coincidence. They are in fact pre-Gyaandostaani names, purely and solely the property of the Republic of Gyaandostaan. To infer otherwise could lead to serious litigation from the Gyaandostaani legal team, who are the only legal team in the world with their own legal team presiding over them—the legal team, that is.

They entered the room one at a time. The first was a guy called Ray Chow. Ray was of Chinese descent. He had come to Gyaandostaan many years ago on a student scholarship. But he lost the college's address on the boat coming over. You see when he heard the ship's alarm go off, he cleared all his pockets, then removed his clothes, and jumped overboard in a bid to save himself. However it wasn't a red alert, but just the call to dinner on deck. By then a highly embarrassed Chow had already hit the water and to compound matters a little more, he didn't know how to swim in the first place and so in fact, ultimately did have to be rescued. This entailed mouth-to-mouth resuscitation provided by a four-foot nine-inch male nurse, as well as a physical examination of all his organs, some of which made it back on deck with him. Chow, having lost all his important documents, along with 8 percent of his self-respect and 59.5 percent of his self-confidence, found himself in a busy bazaar in Gyaandostaan's Bey area. It was here that something really strange happened, a tryst with destiny, something that made him believe that there was a higher power and that power was not a four-foot nine-inch male nurse with saline breath.

He bumped into Jay Huskee. Okay, all right, you caught me, I lied. In fact, Jay Huskee bumped into him. Reversing a Cadillac is never the easiest of tasks, so to do so in a busy bazaar without once even using your car mirrors or tossing your head back can be hazardous. That day Huskee Sr. mowed down 11 people and a kiosk, but none left as strong an impression on him as Chow did. Although it may be said the impression the Cadillac left on Chow was even worse and took seven months to come off.

The car's bumper hit him on the run and Chow went down for the second time in twelve hours. The car proceeded to roll over him in reverse and he ended up in front of the car. Chow looked up and was surprised to see Jay Huskee's awkward expression. Jay was even more surprised to see Chow, as there were no Chinese restaurants in the Bey bazaar area; he presumed the Chinese had invaded Gyaandostaan as they had been threatening to do every alternate weekend. The patriot in him immediately surfaced, and he put both his hands above his head in the universal gesture implying 'I give up'. As he did so, his leg inadvertently pressed the accelerator and promptly ran over Chow again.

It was then that the two men bonded. Well, actually over the whole three-month hospitalization period.

After all, the only man Chow knew in Gyaandostaan was the man who nearly killed him, er...twice.

Once Jay Huskee had got clarification that Chow was not part of a Chinese invading force, vanguard (this was done in the first month itself), he started visiting him in the hospital with an interpreter. Of course, after a month or so, Huskee sacked the interpreter as he realized that Chow spoke perfect Gyaandostaani, and the interpreter was fluent only in French and Russian.

Now Chow's back story is important, not just because we want to sell this book in China, but also because it helps define the relationship between the older Huskee and the younger Chow, going forward. Also, in case we don't mention China again, we really should bore you, the reader, with something.

Huskee would soon become very close to Chow. The relationship would best be described as 'fatherly', though why Huskee thought of Chow as a father figure escaped the comprehension of all political pundits around.

In the course of their bonding in the hospital room, Huskee Sr. offered Chow a job. Chow accepted with one rider—Huskee was never, never to fetch or drop him by car again. Huskee on his part was very impressed with the young Chow. After all, he had survived two accidents, that too in the space of seven seconds. But mostly he was impressed with Chow's most powerful quality—he was Chinese. In a world rocked with recessions and depressions, China alone was swimming against the tide. With Chow in the mix, Jay Huskee had grandiose plans of reviving Gyaandostaan's flagging economy.

The partnership endured and when Huskee eventually became finance minister of Gyaandostaan, Chow became a very powerful figure. Though Chow continued to have an aversion to Cadillacs, he was instrumental in the neo-liberalization policy that brought cheaper Chinese cars into Gyaandostaan's market. Through this, he achieved two important objectives: 1. China made even more money and 2. Cadillacs were quietly phased out of Gyaandostaan.

Paul and Chow hit it off quickly. Chow liked relating to a younger Chow, and Paul finally had someone in the room who was audible.

Shabbir Hoosein was one of those guys who was determined and defined by one feature—he had a very long nose with nose hair spilling out of his nostrils like two grey strands. Shabbir was by profession an accountant, but Jay Huskee loved to have him along as he always created a diversion with his nasal cavity.

The nicest thing anyone said about it of course was to call it the 8th Wonder of the World. However this was a ludicrous suggestion. It quite clearly belonged in the top 7.

Shabbir was a big hit at cocktail parties and social gatherings. Compulsorily, the first half hour would be spent by all the other guests staring at his nose.

He was eventually banned from theatres and cinemas, as when he was in attendance, no one would look at the stage or the screen.

Chow and Shabbir shared a unique relationship. Shabbir would often go to Chow for help on urgent matters. Chow, in turn, would make Shabbir feel special by often hanging his coat on Shabbir's nose, or charging children 3 Ragoos (1 Ragoo is equal to roughly 10 rupees) to pat it ferociously and 5 Ragoos to attempt chin-ups on his nose hair using a tricep grip, palms facing down.

Shabbir had some good ideas though. When Jay Huskee was finance minister and the country was in the throes of a recession, it was he who suggested that all members of team Huskee take a 10 percent cut in their salaries and set an example for the entire nation to follow. It was a novel idea, ahead of its time, and much appreciated by all. Of course, in the end Chow's idea of cutting 50 percent of Shabbir's salary alone is what they went with, as the whole sacrificial method came from Shabbir. The rest of the crew took exactly 25th of a second to vote in favour of this idea. In fact, Chow even said Shabbir should sacrifice 90 percent of his salary to really get the nation's attention, but as by then Shabbir was weeping uncontrollably, they settled at 50 percent.

The 4th pillar was Amama. Now in Gyaandostaan, mama isn't like the western word mamma or momma or momsy or monsticle, neither is it like the Indian word mama which apparently may mean effeminate or affectionate uncle. And when you say A. Mama in Gyaandostaan, you say the whole thing together—Amama—it's a full name.

Amama was a philosopher, a planner. He had the vision which Jay Huskee lacked. He knew what the country needed. It was he who insisted they only hire struggling female ramp models as stenographers, thus fulfilling a social vacuum in the society—providing employment to hundreds of pretty women who couldn't all fit on the few ramps available in the country at the same time, and who weren't prepared to work more than fifty minutes a day in any case.

It was he who came up with the scheme of musical

chairs. For the sum of 5 lakh Ragoos (50 lakh rupees), you could get a chair built on a main road or pavement with the name of your choice on it. And (and this was the USP), when one sat on the chair, your favourite song would play continuously till the chair was vacated. Both the song and the name of the chair was decided by the donor. This worked very well. Initially over 350 chairs were placed all over the streets and pavements of Bey. But after more than a thousand people were injured in accidents in the first ten days itself, the scheme was scrapped. Chairs on a highway, though a great idea, was still way ahead of its time. Its time would only come once cars became extinct—cars or drivers, either one.

That turns us to pillar number 5, the only female in the group—Bella Terrace, known to history as BT.

Bella Terrace was an extremely pretty girl. But that was about 38 years ago. Now she was filled with the aggression and drive you see quite often in women who are at the top of their professions. Social scientist Zakme Beev put it fairly succinctly in his book, *How a Woman is More Like a Man*. Beev explained that women at the top of the heap had an excess of testosterone, which caused them to become very womanlike, very male in their appearance. This manifested itself in the growth of side burns or hair on the lower back and shoulder. They also often walked with a limp, cursed like a sailor, or indulged in upside down standing push-ups during their lunch breaks. Bella did all this and more. Add severe acne and scratching in public, and you have the complete package.

But if you wanted dynamism, Bella was the one. She also had one more credential. She was the niece of the present President—Lt Colonel Jagee.

Now that we've met the Famous Five, let's understand the political beast that prevailed in Gyaandostaan.

Gyaandostaan was, what we political pundits call, a junior democracy or a democracy for juniors, based on the sound principle of democracy and children. How with children do you allow a democratic atmosphere where they can ask questions freely and aren't restrained? Then, if they ask too many questions, they are given detention or locked up, or worse still have their PSPs and iPads confiscated. Also known as democracy with a firm slap, it's the most effective, and dare I say 'egalitarian', form of government going around. Keep in mind 'Democracy' is a fascinating word which has different meanings for different nations. For the Japanese it means freedom. For the North Koreans it's just a long word. For the

Indians it's just something you mention in passing, but never elaborate on. GYAANDOSTAAN? Well, GYAANDOSTAAN was no different.

At this stage, let me share with you some information that was either given to me or occurred to me, I'm not sure which.

In 324 BC, Alexander the Great conquered Gyaandostaan. The people of Gyaandostaan offered resistance to Alexander's commanding forces which lasted all of seven minutes and ended when the Gyaandostaanis tied up their own king from head to toe and offered him to Alexander as an olive branch. The branch broke and the king hurt himself and this caused much mirth among the Macedonians.

So happy was Alexander with this action that instead of killing all the women and children as he had planned, he burnt down all the schools and libraries as a gesture of good faith. Alexander then did what he always did. He named everything after himself. Cities, streets, buildings, colonies were all called Alexander or Myself or Me or Zanders. The influence of Greece and Macedonia is still felt to the present day as Macedonian words like 'Alexander', 'myself', or 'me' are now part and parcel of the Gynaadostaani lingua-franca.

The Gyaandostaanis woke free from the yoke of Macedonian oppression only in the 10th century. Although this was an oversight as no one had told them that the Macedonians had left their shores about 500 years before that. But the influence is still there. For eg. Macedonia and Gyaandostaan are the only two countries in the world where the concept of 'dry' days isn't entertained. A testament to political understanding and civil consciousness of the highest degree.

Alexander himself enjoyed the entire two-week stay in the country. He famously said, 'If there be paradise on earth, then this is not it, but it may be close, somewhere in the nearby vicinity'. Two other quotes on Gyaandostaan are also quoted by him, 'Why are people so short?' and 'The music here has two much treble'. By and large the great man had strange fondness for this country, though due to the staggering effect of red wine, he was never able to correctly pronounce 'GYAANDOSTAAN' in public.

But he left behind a system of governance which evolved into the present Gyaandostaan presidential system. Let's examine this with a fine eye. Failing that, let's examine this any way.

To get a bird's-eye view, or some such thing, let's examine the potential hierarchy through a graph.

At the top sits the president, elected by the people, er... sometimes.

President

↓

a. President's relatives in key coherent positions

↓

b. Friends and business partners, creditors of the President in his past businesses

↓

c. Further flung relatives, pets of the Prez., including goldfish

↓

d. Party workers who have money or are of temporary utilitarian value to the President.

↓

e. All card carrying members of the President's party

Dear reader, this is a good point for you to pick up some other book, because the next portion is rather complicated. In case your still reading, I'll write on. In case you've stopped, I'll write on till you finish reading the other book and come back. Alexander took many wives from GYAANDOSTAAN. He also took two husbands. After some time, he returned the wives. Yet, Alexander's invasion is important as the Macedonian influence will always be part of GYAANDOSTAANI life, even today. It also explains why many GYAANDOSTAANI men wear tunics.

GYAANDOSTAAN'S presidential system had one peculiar tenet—the cabinet wasn't made up of Lt. Colonel Jagee's party members wholly or solely. In fact, the cabinet was a motley crew and included opposition party members, coalition members, assorted relations, and friends. Many of them had no political standing whatsoever. For instance, the agricultural minister was the President's barber. The Prez. was very finicky about his hair. He was the only elderly, non-female President in the world with shoulder length hair, which he often wore in two ponytails. To maintain the perfect length, it had to be trimmed every week. Plus, to keep its lustre, hair products had to be constantly administered. And so Prez. Jagee kept his barber by his side. However, when his advisors said it looked ridiculous that the barber went everywhere with him (swimming pools or saunas being the last straw), the Prez. decided to legitimize the barber's position.

First he decided to create a new ministry, a ministry of hair couture, but his advisors convinced him this would be a silly idea as most of Gyaandostaan subjects would not be able to pronounce the word 'couture'. He then decided to do the rational thing. He went by the alphabet and gave him the first ministry that came up, 'A' for Agricultural.

Elections were held every five years and no president was allowed to stand more than three times i.e. 3 terms. However Lt. Col. Jagee found a way to 4th term through a technicality. He changed his name. For his first 3 terms he served under the name of Rupen Balik. For his 4th term he called himself Jagee, and threw a military title in for good measure as well. Later on, we'll look at Lt. Col. Jagee's military career. For now it's suffice to say that today when your building watchman 'Salaams' you, remember he has more military experience than Lt. Col. Jagee.

After this excruciatingly specific, deep-rooted analysis of the political machinery, I'm sure, dear reader, you will now be able to enjoy this book far more. If not, you will definitely enjoy its sequel. One last thing: there were two large parties that fought for supremacy. One was Lt. Col. Jagee's Sandwich Party which was in power at the present, and in the opposition sat Machado's Ball and Socket Party. Briefly we will look at how these parties came to be.

About 100 years ago, the first political party was started. As rice formed the staple diet of the people, it took the name of the Rice People's Party (RPP). Over many years, it changed names many times but was always loyal to the food products available. The Beetroot People's Republican Army gave way to the Citizens for Currie Change and Cabbage CoConsumption (CCCC) to the Maize Miletial (MM), until finally settling into Lt. Col. Jagee's (at that time Rupen Balik's) Sandwich Party. Jagee explained the name.

The citizens were the meat and cheese in the middle while the government was the two loaves of bread that protected and safeguarded the people. Keep in mind Jagee (then Rupen Balik) spent 15 formative years of his life in merry England, where constant consumption of the sandwich, the only available dish, caused his relationship with the thing to go from excruciatingly bland and repetitive to I've-gotten-so-used-to-it-I-can't-live-without-it. This is the same sort of neoclassical conditioning that one experiences in marriage and long prison terms, thus also explaining the close parallel between all three, i.e., marriage, prison, and sandwiches.

The opposition leader was a close friend of Lt. Col. Jagee who went by the name of M. Machado. They were business partners in almost 70 percent of all large construction works around the country. Machado, in spite of being leader of the opposition, held the portfolio of Public Works Minister in charge of all construction and civic repair work.

For many years there was only one party in Gyaandostaan. It was only 20 years ago that Lt. Col. Jagee (then Rupen Balik), formed the Ball and Socket Party; thus being the only politician to head both opposing political parties in a two-party system in world history. A position that escaped even Hitler.

Hurt by the sniggering of the foreign press, the oversensitive Lt. Col. Jagee, (then Rupen Balik) 'gifted' the party to his business and squash partner, M. Machado. In return Machado was to promise to never to beat him in squash again. We will see later on how M. Machado reneges on his promise. Upto this point also note that M. Machado was not known to have much of a 'backbone'. It's not like he had a great pair of legs either, but he definitely had no backbone.

3

Reader, now that we've set up the story, the action really only starts here. This means three things: 1. It was pointless reading everything up to this point. 2. The publishers should have the good sense to tell you this. 3. I did have the good sense to tell you this.

Our story finally, or rather most finally, begins on the funeral day. It is Jay Huskee's funeral and the family, (meaning Sophia only), has decided to go for an open casket. The setting is the lovely Bollalyo cemetery, at the city's edge. Gyaandostaanis, like most Macedonians, burned their dead sometimes twice. Just to make sure.

On this particular day (since Jay Huskee's body and parking coupons were never found), the open casket has nothing inside except for a small piece of orange cloth, which may or may not be part of an orange saree—no one is sure. And Sophia wanted to keep it that way.

Since no one was clear on whether Jay Huskee was a nice enough man, the eulogy was delivered by Mr D'Souza. As not a soul understood a word, this question was safely tackled. But our story starts with the chance encounter between President Lt. Col. Jagee and Paul Huskee—heir apparent to the Huskee throne.

Like all good politicians, Lt. Col. Jagee timed himself perfectly. He reached the funeral just as it ended. Jagee was dressed in all his finery. Ever since he had promoted himself to the rank of colonel, he was forever dotting his crisp white uniform with various medals. Though no one dared to ask him how he had Britain's Victoria Cross, Germany's Iron Cross, and Gyaandostaan's Blue Cross all at the same time. Jagee carried the customary white handkerchief and dark glasses, which helped him and many celebrities hide their absolute lack of empathy to those around them. Jagee's security detail went straight to Paul.

Soon Bella Terrace, Paul, and Col. Jagee huddled in a corner where everyone could see them. Colonel Jagee decided to get on with investiture ceremony, right then and there at the funeral.

In Gyaandostaani political tradition, the person who inherits a seat is sworn in through a symbolic manner in which he actually sits on a ceremonial seat

Jagee was dressed in all his finery. Ever since he had promoted himself to the rank of colonel, he was forever dotting his crisp white uniform with various medals.

and then swears allegiance to the government and the country. A seat was brought in and Paul was placed on it, thus completing the formalities. Unfortunately, since the seat had been freshly painted, Paul took about 15 minutes to get out of it. Meanwhile revelry broke out, with supporters of the Sandwich Party opening bottles of champagne. Thus the funeral turned out ironically to be a rather gay occasion. Jay Huskee would have been proud.

The next day is when Paul's life changed forever.

This is finally where our story starts, dear reader. This time I kid you not. I know we've been through a lot together, you and I. But you mustn't lose the faith. There have been false starts in plenty, I admit, but this is finally final. The story starts with Paul entering President Lt. Col. Jagee's office. This is where we begin. Finally. I think.

As the Famous Five entered Col. Jagee's bungalow, this is what they saw.

A large hall had 27 pictures of Col. Jagee displayed on its walls. All youthful. In all he was V-shaped and trim. In real life Col. Jagee was on the lighter side. The lighter side of 300 pounds. At the end of the hall was a large red door. As the five went through, they were ushered into Col. Jagee's gym. A word about Col. Jagee (to save time, we may drop the 'Lt.'). Jagee was a vain man, a strange man, and a large man. To understand his character, you must first understand that this was a man who declared himself a Colonel and now had four Generals reporting to him! His point 'What is good enough for Gaddafi is good enough for me' must be noted.

Col. Jagee was wearing a tight underwear and yellow shoes. As he saw them enter, he quietly put on his glasses and climbed on to the treadmill. Then he motioned Paul to get on to the treadmill next to his. Paul was worried that he may have to also get into his underwear to fit in, but luckily for him that didn't happen. As they ran, Col. Jagee started speaking. His stomach was bouncing off his body at an alarming speed. All eyes were transfixed on him. 'Paul, I need you to take on the Finance Minister's mantle. Your grandfather had it, and I only took it away from him because of his fiendish dressing and obsession with the colour orange. Let's make this a prosperous country. We need your youthful exuberance. The finance ministry needs your energy and dynamism. What do you say?'

Col. Jagee was wearing a tight underwear and yellow shoes. As he saw them enter, he quietly put on his glasses and climbed on to the treadmill.

As the Famous Five exited quite satisfied, with the eyes upwards, the bouncing belly thundered, 'Oh yes, Paul, there is that small matter of our fiscal deficit which is 3,200 crore Ragoos. You need to deal with that first.' As they walked out of the room, Paul almost vomited. He only stopped because Shabbir Hossein actually did throw up, just under a portrait of Col. Jagee hugging Abraham Lincoln at Gettysburg. Or at least they thought it was Gettysburg because Lincoln had never come to GYAANDOSTAAN.

Paul was in a bind. 3,200 crore Ragoos! 48 hours earlier, his problem was whether to order in for a Chinese or Thai meal? Suddenly his problem had been elevated into how to wipe off a country's 3,200 crore Ragoos deficit?

I think by now it's fair to say, our story starts in Paul's new office, where the Famous Five are in a huddle in which, along with trying to avoid being hit by Shabbir Hossein's nose, they are desperately coming to terms with a hopeless situation. Hossein quickly outlined the situation. Money was owed mostly to the twice-a-week Democratic Republic of China, a little was owed to the World Bank, and an even smaller sum to Canada. It's the Chinese who were looking for their sweet-and-sour pound of flesh and who had tightened the focus on Col. Jagee.

Ray Chow was the most positive. He came out with a four-pronged action plan:

1 Increase taxes and duties substantially.
2. Find new businesses and avenues.
3. Borrow more money to pay off the 'borrowed' money, possibly from friendly countries like the US, Germany, or even India.
4. Run away from Gyaandostaan when Col. Jagee is sleeping, never to return.

As the emotions died down, better sense prevailed, and all five decided to go with option 4. Amama started doing the booking for East Timor, everyone's favoured choice for relocation.

At this point, Bella Terrace had one of those moments that define human history. You know like when Hannibal crossed the Alps or King John signed the Magna Carta. She sneezed. The sneeze was so loud that everyone seemed to have their senses returned to them, with immediate effect. This allowed the group to think clearly once again. Though obviously no one wanted to sit next to Bella Terrace.

Amama was the first to get to the point. 'East Timor has a very bad winter and very little night life. We must think objectively here; I say we go to the Canary Islands.' Only Paul looked incredulous. In his mind, he wondered whether this really is the 'crack group' that could steer Gyaandostaan to safety. At a time like this, leaders are tested. Paul was no different.

His team needed guidance, vision, a ray of light. Then suddenly it came to Paul—the answer, the solution, the formula to wipe out all their troubles. 'Let's drink,' he said. And so, against the back of a debt of 3,200 crore Ragoos, the festivities began.

Paul, again displaying his leadership role, was the first to take off his pants.

The obvious games followed. Suggestions had to be given to wipe off the deficit. If the rest didn't agree with the suggestion, the 'suggestor' had to drink a double shot of vodka. Luckily, Jay Huskee, while he did a little for the exchequer, also did a little for his vodka collection. He had many different brands, all with Russian names, and none actually from Russia. There was 'Ya Snaayu' from Nepal, 'Vladeevanious' from Cuba, 'Cobaka' from Naples, and 'Bolshoi Bullet' from Bulgaria. In fact there was so much vodka that Bella Terrace suggested they start selling some of it to aid the effort against the deficit. She got a double shot for her trouble. However, when Bella Terrace started dropping her pants, Amama firmly believed there was not enough vodka available in the world to digest this particular sight, and in a burst of creativity, he offered that they give Col. Jagee to China as a gift. This brought the room to a standstill. Even Ray Chow, who was wearing Shabbir Hoosein's pants draped around his neck like a scarf, seemed to warm to the idea. A pantless Bella Terrace, who was trying to convince Amama to come out from under the desk in which he was hiding, liked the idea so much that in the interest of collective harmony and world peace she agreed to put her pants back on.

We must leave Paul and the Famous Five alone to enjoy their drink, as that is the gentlemanly thing to do, and look at their urgent political matter that seemed to be developing.

The Ball and Socket Party had an unusual visitor on Tuesday afternoon. Don't ask me which Tuesday afternoon, because I don't have a calendar in front of me, so it could have been any Tuesday afternoon. Actually, it could have been a Wednesday or even a Thursday afternoon.

Okay, so one Friday afternoon, Machado was busy at work in his ridiculously large office, when he received a visitor. Now by 'busy at work' I mean he was busy playing video games, since work for Machado meant whatever instruction Col. Jagee gave him. Today he was playing Hit Boss, a ridiculously violent game that seemed unsuitable for adults as it involved no nudity whatsoever. Machado was hard at it. He had in fact just kicked the boss when his phone rang. It was his secretary who seemed quite irate as she had been disturbed by the visitor just when she was about to scale a win, her third in a row, in a game called Angry Birds.

Machado didn't want to answer the phone. If he did, he'd land up losing his momentum and invariably lose his winning position as well.

So the leader of the opposition ignored the persistent buzzer.

Then he suddenly looked across his desk and found Colleen Connor standing there.

Dear reader, at this point you must have turned to your near and dear ones and asked them one of the two things—Do you have Angry Birds, and, or, who is Colleen Connor?

Colleen Connor's story was a little like Ray Chow's, the difference being she was one inch taller. And possibly female. Colleen was born in Ireland, but as her father was a diplomat, she came to live in Bey,

Gyaandostaan, from the age of 13. Now, twenty years later, she was 100 percent Gyaandostaani.

She had made quite a name for herself as a champion for women's rights and the downtrodden, which she discovered were one and the same thing. Her accomplishments were many.

For instance, a member of the legislature had beaten up a couple of women at a toll booth. Apparently, the women manning (excuse the term) the toll booth didn't show him enough respect. They should have been standing, instead they were seated. What he didn't know is that the ceiling of the toll booth was real low—so if they stood up, they'd hit their heads. Consequently, sitting was the only option.

The brave MLA, in any case, was aghast at this slight to his position and was completely clueless to the operator's position. Putting his life in great danger, he charged into the booth along with three bodyguards and then initiated a bout of hair pulling. A game he was clearly cheating at as the only hair on his head was in his ears.

It was Colleen Connor who led the investigation against the minister. She famously called him a 'boob'. The name stuck and he was now called the 'boob' minister. He was forced to resign under public and media pressure, and though he was quietly reinstated in two months, his new moniker followed him around, much to his chagrin. Recently, the 'boob' minister was given the portfolio of Women Upliftment and Child Development—a ministry which he clearly was cut out for. Whenever in GYAANDOSTAAN there was a wife beating, molestation, or sexism case, Colleen and her band of ferocious females were there in full fighting finery. Many males were impaled on their swords.

'I'll come straight to the point.'

Machado looked up to see the source of the sentence. It was Colleen Connor who was standing over his desk. Machado was one of those men who were very nervous around women. He immediately started sweating and stuttering.

'I've got a proposition for you,' Colleen continued unabated.

'But...but...I'm...I...I...I'm already married,' Machado protested under incredible strain.

'Don't be an absolute moron. Try to keep up please, I have a political proposition which may interest you, Machado,' said Colleen.

Machado felt he had stopped breathing completely. *Why did she have to say my name out aloud?* he wondered fearfully. As his breath became shorter, he tried clearing air in front of his face in a gesture which mimicked someone swimming the breast stroke on land. ' I'm not feeling too...too...too good...too good,' he gasped. As he sputtered out the sentence, he started to blow air into his chest with his dry, pursed lips.

'Someone has to stop that fascist nutcase Jagee and I think that person should be you,' thundered Colleen.

Machado actually collapsed. Take on Colonel Jagee, his provider? Machado's head hit his desk with a sickening thud. Machado hoped of course that he was finally dead. However, his tie got caught in the desk drawer, instantly choking him and simultaneously convincing him that he was staying alive, despite his own best efforts.

'It's time you behaved like a true opposition leader. You've played the lap dog too long,' provoked Colleen Connor sarcastically.

'But, but, but I make a good...good...lap...lap dog.' Machado's mouth had by now seceded from the rest of his body and decided to fly solo. To compensate for this inability to expire, Machado also found his hands covering his eyes. He tried some visualization techniques, like thinking of something terrible to induce death, but all he could come up with was the omelette he had had for breakfast which he felt was much smaller than his usual omelettes, and he needed to have a word with the wife, except that the last time he tried such a thing, she threatened to fry an egg on his head. Try as hard as he did, this thought did not have the ultimate effect and led to death. It, in fact, only led to more depression.

Ignoring this personification of regression, Colleen Conner continued,- 'We need to save Gyaandostaan. We need real democracy. Jagee must go and the Ball and Socket Party must become a true opposition. Take him on and eventually bring him down.'

On hearing these words, Machado fell off his chair, onto the floor, and eventually started crying. From that position, on his knees, he looked up at Colleen Connor and excused himself on health grounds.

'I'm...I'm to have a gall...gall...gall bladder operation next month. My doctor says I shouldn't do anything...anything...strenuous.' With the effort required in passing on this information, he fell on his side.

'That's why I'm offering you a positive solution. We'll join hands to form a coalition and bring him down together, since it's abundantly clear that you are incapable of standing up on your own,' Colleen offered.

Funny she should say that, Machado thought, as

standing upright was what he was desperately trying to do at that point. Clinging to the table, he pushed himself back up into a more 'homo sapien' position. 'Jagee will kill me', was meekly emitted by a voice which was now clearly on its last legs.

Colleen Connor knew she had him. She changed her stance. She slowly patted him down onto his chair and changed her tone to a more supportive, motherly one. She reassured him and placated him. His reaction, of course, could not be authenticated accurately as by then Machado had slipped into 'rigor mortis'.

Colleen spelt it out. R.I.G.O.R. M.O.R.T.I.S. Oh no, sorry, Colleen spelt out her basic strategy. Apparently Col. Jagee's success over the past few years had led to a lot of added weight in the shape of arrogance. There were plenty of skeletons to be gleaned from the cupboards. It would be an all-out dog fight, but Colleen felt she had enough on the President to ensure that there would be only one winner. She spoke of solidarity. She spoke of unity. She spoke of championing a cause. Gaining collective strength by a unified stand, she put a hand on Machado's shoulder and asked him to reach in and show fortitude.

By now Machado didn't seem to have a pulse. All movement had stopped. It was as if Colleen was speaking to separate body parts who collectively couldn't function. The next 24 hours were going to be vital. Not just to see if he would breathe again but to see what Machado's various body parts were going to do with all the information.

Colleen Connor left the office knowing that the seeds had been sown. Of course, having chosen as a partner an animal without any vertebrae whatsoever, forget backbone, she had the odds stacked against her. Be that as it may, the first step had been taken. But what would he feed the hand that slaps him? This was the question. Of course these GYAANDOSTAANI proverbs do lose a little in the translation.

4

The next day parliament was in session and all the cats were on prowl. Gyaandostaan had only one house system of parliament called the 'Bigger House' when loosely translated from the original Gyaandostaani word. When tightly translated, it becomes a metaphor for Bubonic plague from medieval Europe. So let's stick with the loose translations.

Technically, members of parliament were elected from constituencies all over Gyaandostaan. Then the party with the majority in parliament formed the government. Colonel Jagee, however, changed this system from election to appointment. People still went through the grind of standing, contesting, and getting elected. He then naturally ignored the whole process and appointed whoever he chose fit to be in the parliament. He explained checks and balances in his monumental biography ghost written by himself (through the eyes of a colonel) as 'the balance of power is controlled by the one who controls the cheques'. Colonel Jagee was so happy with his effort that he gave himself the Gyaandostaan Man Booker Prize; he also nominated himself for a Noble Prize in Economics, The Balkan Palm, The Associated Press Star, and a few Pulitzers.

At that time, the Sandwich Party had 152 seats out of a total of 300. The Ball and Socket Party had about 94. The remaining 54 seats were divided amongst independents and powerful celebrities. About 5 percent were not contested as nobody lived in those remote constituencies. Most of the celebrity MPs were Jagee's friends, business partners, or family members. Half the independent members were his employees. Thus, almost the whole of parliament was under his thumb. This could be summed up as 'Jagee having more power than Hitler, but little less than a young Margaret Thatcher'. Parliament started at 9 am that day. Col. Jagee outlined the agenda.

Agenda

9 o'clock: Breakfast

10 o'clock: Paul Huskee to address House on Deficit

11 o'clock: Brunch

12 o' clock: Machado to ask unimportant questions that are to be easily answered. Thus, quelling the opposition

1 o'clock: Lunch

2 o'clock: Siesta

3.30: Question hour (this question hour is not to run more than 20 minutes)

4 o'clock: Tea and snacks

5 o'clock: Closing message from Prez.

5.30: Drinks and supper

5.55: National Anthem (standing optional)

Normally, question hour was a quick process. Questions asked of the government varied from 'Can we have a longer lunch break?' to 'Should larger TV screens be installed in parliament during important football matches?'. In fact, the only controversial question asked of the government in the last few years was when one member of the opposition asked whether members of parliament should be entitled to three parking spaces each.

However, this resulted in the parking spaces being increased to four per MP. Thus, a happy result from a tricky question.

Yet, on this day in question, the question hour was to 'experience' her finest moment. In all fairness, it seemed an innocuous question, hardly likely to bring down the government. Keep in mind that dissent or even plain curiosity had never been able to flourish in these hallowed halls.

Machado couldn't explain how it happened. In the last 57 years of his life, he had experienced courage only twice—once when he agreed to marry his wife who was choking his neck with both hands at the time, and second when he saw her for the first time, which really should have been the first time. However, the moment the President opened the question hour, some force seemed to overtake him. At first, he thought it was his insulin injection that caused him to stand up. Then, having stood up, he hoped it was to close the zip that he often left undone. Finally, he hoped the National Anthem would resound.

The President benignly asked 'Yes Machado, you have a question?' Bear in mind that Machado had spoken only once before in parliament over the last 5 years, and that was simply to seek permission to use the toilet.

'If it's about the toilet, didn't you go yesterday'? the President continued to loud laughter. Machado and Col. Jagee had an interesting relationship. The Col. used him as a punching bag—he'd roll out the jokes and the public would laugh. Machado would seem impervious, except for his chronic sweating. But this afternoon something changed. Machado cut into the laughter, 'I was thinking shouldn't the question hour be for a full 60 minutes and not just 20?'

Pin drop silence followed.

Machado couldn't believe what he had just said. He tried to sit but his legs failed him. He tried to stop the words from coming out of his mouth using both hands, but words are not physical things and can't be held back once released. Words also have few principles—once freed, they turn their back on you and leave you to deal with the consequences, while they carry on about their merry way. Machado was disgusted with them. He made a note to himself that once disentangled from this present mess, he'd never ever use words again.

'Okay, here's a thought Machado. We'll use the full 60 minutes. 20 minutes will be for the questions, and the next 40 minutes, you could perhaps do a performance for the parliament. You know, a poem, or a skit, a song, maybe a tribal dance? What about holding an aerobics class?' Laughter resumed at the President's comments.

'I'll start dancing when Gyaandostaan is out of

debt and on her feet again.' Machado tried hard to swallow his own tongue, but the words, having tasted freedom, were unstoppable. Machado, just to make sure, checked with his finger to see if his tongue was still in his mouth. But the damage was done. At the last comment, Col. Jagee flew out of his chair. He couldn't digest this flagrant show of defiance, not to mention betrayal. The way he saw it, he owned Machado, who shouldn't breathe a word without his Excellency's permission.

'Are you blatantly criticizing my government?' Jagee flungst Machado. Each word said separately and deliberately.

'No I'm just saying that the country is falling apart. We are in debt up to our necks, and you, as a leader of the house, want to initiate dance sessions! Your solution to a fiscal deficit of 3,200 crore Ragoos is aerobics sessions? Seems a bit strange.'

By now, Col. Jagee had turned purple. He had initially gone a beetroot red, but now, anger, indignity, exasperation, and social embarrassment, not to mention defiance of his authority, meant the only outcome was to turn purple.

Let's leave this incident here because this really is the point at which our story must begin. A tale is only a tale when conflict is made perfectly clear. By standing up to Col. Jagee, Machado gives us a final (absolutely swear on my mother), final beginning to this chronicle. We now know that this story is about two things—a. forces in Gyaandostaan fighting for power and b. people occasionally turning purple.

When Machado left the parliament, the battle lines were drawn. Machado didn't like it, but he knew he was powerless. Colleen Connor had obviously hypnotized him, and now he was ready to bite the hand that fed him and the mouth that made fun of him. The mouth itself was in deep shock, and was unprepared for this outcome. Col. Jagee had created a pseudo opposition, never envisaging they may actually, one day, oppose. If he had some warning of this turn of events, he may even have been able to choose another colour. Purple was too conspicuous and eye catching, quite frankly, thus making it a day in parliament no one was ever likely to forget. As Machado walked out of the hall in pin drop silence, Col. Jagee made a mental note to himself—*Challenge me? As soon as possible I'll have the toilets closed.*

Machado's office the next day had a grim look about it. Similar feelings must have been felt on the Titanic fifteen minutes before she went under water. Machado spent a lot of time in the bathroom. Possibly three and half of the first six hours. This was because the office lines kept ringing and Machado didn't want to appear to be a liar when his PA would tell Col. Jagee's PA that the boss was in the bathroom. The first 27 times Jagee's man called was okay, but by the 28th call, Col. Jagee's PA started suspecting mischief was afoot. So he tried another tact. He'd regulate his voice and call under certain pseudonyms. Among those attempted were the carpenter, Machado's third grade teacher Mrs Almeida, Machado's third grade teacher Mrs Almeida's son (to say Mrs Almeida had just died), the Queen of England, the Queen's mother, Mohammad Ali, Mohammad Ali's mother, JK Rowling and her mother... But, Machado was constant in his cowardice (an admittedly average quality). If the phone rang, he just sprung towards the bathroom, and that was that. Colleen Connor in the meantime walked right into Machado's office in the middle of the day with various newspapers, all carrying the triumph and glory—her triumph and her glory.

The *Gyaandostaani Express* headline read,

'Machado does a Neil Amstrong, takes first step on the moon'. The *GT* (*Gyaandostaan Times*) screamed 'Machado to release new book titled *POLITICAL SUICIDE'*.

The *Statesperson*'s headline was 'Rare Iguana species found in Gyaandostaan'. However, this was because the newspaper had become a nature journal and didn't cover politics. *Unkind Critics* of course said the *Statesperson*'s headline was a veiled reference to Col. Jagee, who had in the past been called far worse things than an Iguana, including names of various fruits, Emperor Penguins, and 'Col. Jagee' itself.

When Colleen entered his office, Machado was in the lavatory. On overhearing the phone conversation, Colleen grabbed the receiver form Machado's PA and shrieked into the phone.

'Please tell your President that if he wishes to speak to the leader of the opposition, he needs to make an appointment like anyone else. I'm sure we'll be able to squeeze him in sometime after next Wednesday, and please stop calling incessantly. Unlike you people, we are trying to save a country here! Miraculously, the calls stopped after her tirade. Ultimately, the sheer ferocity of the female species will always prevail. Meanwhile, Machado was safely ensconced in his private chair and although Colleen was the lesser of the two evils, he was in no hurry to come out his comfort zone.

Finally, he was coaxed out with a cup of hot milk and two biscuits. Machado was still in a daze when Colleen laid into him.

Machado perhaps thought it would be a frosty reaction as his actions has invited a street battle. However, Colleen instead hugged him so passionately that Machado could have sworn he heard a rib crack, though it may also have been the second indigested biscuit. Who could tell for sure?

Colleen Connor made her pleasure be known to all and sundry. She was a passionate woman, very Irish in her straightforwardness. And bear in mind straightforwardness had not yet been invented in Gyaandostaan. So, while she hugged Machado tight, for Machado's part, nothing happened. Machado had experienced a hug only twice before in his life. Once, on his 5th birthday from his then father (Machado's mother married 11 times), and in the eighth grade, when his friend Putin was trying to mimic a boa constrictor with its prey. Machado became the prey, despite all his animated plea not to volunteer for the role.

Colleen went on to outline that now that the battle lines had been drawn, the politics had to begin. They

While she (Colleen) hugged Machado tight, for Machado's part, nothing happened. Machado had experienced a hug only twice before in his life.

needed to make the Ball and Socket Party into a real combative force. In her words, 'More Ball, less Socket.'

Ninety percent of the Bigger House was at the moment with Col. Jagee. She had it off the record, plus one, ie. off, off the record, that at least 10–15 percent of the MPs were more than happy with Machado's challenge and could be easily swayed to gravitate towards the opposition. Jagee's arrogance would now cost him. Once the new numbers became clear, the hard battle towards swaying the rest must begin. Colleen pointed out that Rome wasn't built in a day. Machado countered that to his knowledge they were actually given only a week. His PA explained that in those days, people used to work on weekends as well. Colleen replied 'One week built Rome, one year we'll build Gyaandostaan.' Machado said, 'Why not meet halfway? Take 6 months and build Rome instead?' Colleen gave him such a glare that Machado ran with great fear to the toilet. Three seconds later, his PA followed suit.

Colleen dragged them out, reminded Machado that he now was a 'real' leader, and having sat them down, outlined her plans. But just to be on the safer side, she had the bathroom door locked from the outside. Twice.

Paul was now the defacto head of finance. His crack

team, full of cracks. His boss Col. Jagee seemed to be more Mussolini and less Kennedy with every passing day. To make matters worse, Jagee had asked Paul to undertake a very delicate task.

Miffed by the disrespect, slighted by the refusal to answer the phone, Jagee wanted Paul to go as an emissary to the Ball and Socket office, and deliver a veiled threat to Machado that he should toe party line, go over to Col. Jagee and apologize, and pay a fine of 300 crore Ragoos to the Sandwich Party. In fact, Jagee's letter to Machado read as this,

'Oye bloody Machado,

Enough is enough. Ingratitude must also have its limits. However, it's come to my notice that you are being forced into this erratic behavior by your refusal to take your medication on time, and because of some other outside, foreign influence. Let me remind you, the yellow pills are to be taken eight times a day, the blue ones are to be taken four times, and the cod liver oil is to be consumed first thing in the morning, on an empty stomach. I also hereby fine you 300 crore Ragoos for your infantile public outburst. The punishment must include a written apology in Macedonian, handing over your summer villa outside Bey, your entire Bee Gees record collection, your

> *yellow tunic, all your socks, and a poem, written entirely by you explaining why you are such a waste to society and how you'd never challenge my authority, again. You will find that since I'm in a good mood, you are getting off lightly. So strike fast while the iron is hot, and save what's left of your life and career.*

It was undersigned 'The one' for some inexplicable reason.

Paul didn't like the job. He was supposed to be finance minister. Now he'd been demoted to postman.

We now come to a very important stage in our story, a point at which we can get our ship to sail. Eventually, all roads must lead to Rome. A stitch in time saves nine. Where there's a will there's a way. At the point at which Paul Huskee climbs the steps of the main atrium of the Ball and Socket Party's office, our story, our tale, our song, our love ballad, begins anew, at last.

Yes folks, we now come to the inevitable beginning of our tale, I kid you not, and can lie to you no more.

Paul walked past the questioning security officer in a way only seasoned Gyaandostaani politicians can. The trick here was to treat all the security detail with absolute contempt, like they never existed. Mere fleas, not even worth a scratch. Hence no query of theirs was entertained. And not even a cursory glance was thrown their way and wasted on them. He brushed past all uniforms and strode confidently into the main office chamber. Paul didn't like what he was doing, but that didn't mean he wouldn't do it in style.

Huddled around an oval table was a large black violin case, which later Paul realized was Machado himself, but it was the figure opposite the violin case that immediately caught his eye. Colleen O'Connor wasn't a natural beauty, but she had a certain presence, a certain aura, which could slowly ensnare the observer, i.e., she wasn't the type of femme fatale you fell in love with in fifteen minutes, but if you looked fifteen minutes, then she had you. But in Paul's case things wound up a little different.

Paul had one look at Colleen and figured he'd died and gone to heaven. Only the presence of the crumpled violin case in the same frame made him doubt, ever so slightly, this assumption.

As he walked towards them in a daze, Paul thought he was looking at a never-ending cascade of hair bouncing off the most beautiful head he had ever seen outside of the Gyaandostaani National Museum.

Perhaps this is why he didn't quite see Machado's Personal Assistant's right foot, which came into contact with his own heel, causing him to miss a step, stumble, and land in a heap at Colleen's feet. And what pretty feet they were, complete with 5 toes each. Every one a beauty. Each with its own separate nail! Each nail, with its own separate nail polish. And each nail had such a symmetrical design, as never been seen before on human foot. Although, Paul had, truth be told, never really looked at anybody else's feet before, ever, except on a holiday in France. And frog legs was more about legs than feet.

'Ah Paul Huskee, decided to defeat Mr Machado?' said an Irish accent with a heavy Gyaandostaani twang.

Paul immediately suffered a mild seizure. 'She said my name, she said my name.' Unfortunately, as happens to people in delirium, he said his thoughts out aloud. Machado and the PA, moved by their fear which caused one to become a crumpled violin case and the other to merge with the floor, immediately snapped into rapt attention. Meanwhile Paul, realizing he had been heard, tried to save face. 'She said my name! How dare she say my name?' But he wasn't fooling anyone. The wry grin on Colleen's face meant she sensed an opportunity. 'Only your master can call you by name, is it?' she chided. Paul vehemently went on to explain that Col. Jagee was not his master, and that he had no master. And how he was one who could never have a master, and if he did, it would never ever be Col. Jagee because he always envisioned his master to be way shorter.

He let his words take effect. Then, after a minute's silence, he pulled out the letter and said, 'Col. Jagee sent me with a letter for Mr Machado. Please sign here for verification that you have read it. If you don't sign, Col. Jagee will be very, very angry with me.' The last two words were a whisper. So saying, Paul slumped into the chair and wore the expression of a man who had just been run over by a train, which is a mighty clear example of when missing a train is actually a good thing.

Colleen realized she had a golden opportunity to make inroads into Col. Jagee's court via this young man. This she did by one single act. She put her hand on Paul's shoulder. Paul felt as if he was hit by the train again. Which sounds pretty foolish if you think about it—two trains hitting you consecutively one after another, in a span of three minutes. But this time he enjoyed being hit by the train. In fact, he couldn't wait for the train to hit him again, so much so that he screamed, 'Train, train come back!' the moment she took her hand off him. Since the words had been once again conveyed out aloud, Machado and his PA were convinced that Paul Huskee was suffering from the same mental illness as his grandfather had before him. Machado quickly told his PA to lock up all the windows in the building. Can't have a Huskee flying out of one of their windows now, can we?

The next one hour was the most important hour in the political life of Gyaandostaan. Paul and Colleen chatted and Colleen convinced Paul that he was with the wrong party and the wrong leader. This she did not accomplish with long, sensible, thought-provoking speeches, but by simply putting her hand on his shoulders or thigh from time to time. Paul agreed to all her points simply because after a while he wasn't really listening. He was just watching her lips move and found them to be so captivating that he wanted to build a home between them and live there for the rest of his life. He couldn't decide which lip was prettier, the upper or the lower.

Mr Machado, realizing that too much heat was being produced in the room, did what all crumpled violin cases do when they are incompatible. He moved base into the bathroom, where he was accompanied by an utterly confused PA.

5

Now our story deserves a real impetus. This can come from borrowing a plot from another story or by finding an event that actually kick-starts the action. Since I'm unable to do either, let's just meander quietly to Bella Terrace's 50th birthday celebration, held at a glam suburban 5-star hotel that looks like the Taj, sounds like the Taj, but turns out to be Gyaandostaani for Taj, the Taj Hotel of Gyaandostaan. Bella Terrace had some major entertainment on the cards. First up was an Uzbeki Gymnast, Natalia, who could pirouette while swallowing whole tennis balls, after which, for Act Two, she somersaulted and regurgitated the balls. Shabbir Hoosein, who was an amateur Unani Physician and had consumed 2½ bottles of some poor tasting vodka, sensing the woman was in trouble, threw her down and tried pumping her belly to push the balls out. Natalia turned out to be an even better pugilist than a gymnast. Her fists pumelled Shabbir Hoosein into submission. Amama, thinking his friend was being attacked (which he was), mounted the gymnast in a bid to stop her from killing his friend, who was now lying comatose below her. Amama, whose weight is roughly equivalent to two mosquitoes and a little less than one house fly, soon found himself being squashed between Natalia and Shabbir Hoossein.

Ray Chow now dived in to stop the massacre. However, when the birthday girl herself was being roughed up in the quest to retrieve Natalia's balls, the police were called. The party came to a standstill and the police, after questioning a few people, decided to arrest Bella Terrace. She immediately made some phone calls and the police officer in question was suspended and transferred to a desk job. As you can see, this was entertainment at its finest. But all this was just a precursor to the main act that was still to come. That act started at 1:45 pm, way after Natalia's acts, way after the police left, and way after Paul Huskee had finished his fifth vodka. The first three were consumed for himself, the next two were consumed so that he could chat with Colleen. However, at quarter to midnight, the banter in the room stopped at the sight of eight bodyguards with machine guns. Eight bodyguards dressed like traders in ill-fitting safari suits. They heralded the entrance of the President of Gyaandostaan, Bella's uncle—Col. Jagee. The president had perfected a ferocious look for public events.

He had watched a lot of footage of Saddam Hussein as well as Benito Mussolini and mixed up their serious harsh expressions, thus developing one of his own. Saddam's was fairly straightforward. His expression was all moustache which was quickly successfully adopted by Col. Jagee. Benito's was a different cup of tea. He had that transfixed, mad look of a hungry hamster. Benito also had a few tics such as a shaking eye and quivering lips. Marrying all these different factors together meant Col. Jagee's public persona was quite a show. It included a harsh, sombre moustache, coupled with a stare down, then an eye that twitched, alternating with cheeks that swelled up. This is probably how he earned the sobriquet 'bull frog', one that was never yet discussed to his face. As Jagee made his entry, he raised his hand like Julius Caesar and then after 5 full seconds dropped it, a gesture that conveyed that he wanted the cacophony in the room to resume, which it did. It was at this point that Paul Huskee, deep in conversation with Colleen Connor, was momentarily distracted by what he began to think was an extremely large, overgrown bull frog gesturing wildly at him.

Col. Jagee had heard rumours about possible dissent, and the best way to show everyone who was top dog, sorry top frog, was to publicly confront the rumours. And so the bull frog advanced, more Mussolini of troubles, less Saddam and moustaches, toward Paul Huskee.

'Get me a whiskey soda, Huskee,' Jagee commanded. There was no response. A kind of hush hit the room, reminiscent of a saloon in the Wild West when one gunslinger challenged another. 'Huskee, I'm talking to you,' said a voice so chilling that nobody picked up the Italian accent that had mysteriously landed up under the chilling tone.

'What?' replied Paul Huskee. Now there was panic in the room, not from the word itself, but the disrespectful way in which it was delivered.

'Fetch me a whiskey and make it quick,' continued a voice that was half Colonel Jagee and half Benito Mussolini, probably a Benito Jagee, according to unconfirmed reports.

'Absolutely not. I'm busy. There's the bar, go fetch it yourself.' Paul found that 5 vodkas and the attention

He (Col. Jagee) had watched a lot of footage of Saddam Hussein as well as Benito Mussolini and mixed up their serious harsh expressions, thus developing one of his own.

of a lady love would make a Chengiz Khan out of any man, even a Huskee.

'What did you say'? Col. Jagee's delivery was no longer Italian or Iraqi. He was simply breathless with exasperation, typical Col. Jagee on the treadmill.

'I said fetch it yourself. Oh, and one more thing...' Paul stopped and stared at the glowering president. 'Get me a vodka soda while you are at it.'

With this one sentence, Paul Huskee declared war on Col. Jagee, President elect of all Gyaandostaan.

There was an audible gasp from the collective audience. The bull frog puffed out his chest and said, 'Son, if you don't fetch me my drink in the next ten seconds, you'll be expelled from the party.'

Paul replied, 'Which party?'

CJ: 'The party you're in.'

PH: 'But this isn't your party.'

CJ: 'But it is my party, you idiot. You're in my party.'

PH: 'No, I'm in Bella Terrace's party. You are in her party.'

CJ: 'No, she's in her party, I'm in my party, and you are in my party and not in her party.'

PH: 'Actually I'm in her party, she's in her party, and neither of us are in your party.'

CJ: 'I'm in MY party, you are in MY party, and she's

welcome to my party.'

PH: 'If you are in your party, then what are you doing here in her party? You can't be in your party and her party at the same time.'

CJ: 'But I'm NOT in her party. I'm in my party, you are in my party. Ray Chow, whose party is Huskee in?'

Ray Chow: 'You are in her party, he's in her party, she and me are also in her party, so frankly no one knows who is in your party?'

This was the coup de grâce.

A giggle perforated in the room. Col. Jagee had just lost an important verbal skirmish. He tried to win some faux points as the ship went down through. 'Huskee, Chow, you are both thrown out of my party.'

PH: 'For the love of God it is not your party, it's her party, so you can't throw anyone out as it isn't your party.' Now the room burst out, and President Jagee had lost. He had been verbally defeated and humiliated. Public dissent and ridicule is the worst thing that can happen to a politician after failed bariatric surgery.

His minders and bodyguards ushered the irate, but crumpled, bull frog out of the room. But the worst thing that could have happened, happened. Not only was Jagee's power dented publicly, and that too possibly forever, he didn't even get his drink. As it turned out, it really wasn't his party!

The euphoria after President Jagee left was unbelievable. No one in the room realized how unpopular he was until he actually left. The party (and by this party, let me first make it abundantly clear that I'm talking about Bella Terrace's 50th birthday party here) was mixed with guests from both parties and all political streams. Yet the cheering that followed Jagee's exit was similar to the one that followed Mussolini's exit (Mussolini exited politics with grace and poise, hanging from a streetlight for hours, if you recall). Paul Huskee had not just made a political statement of sorts, he had vanquished the President in a high pitched battle, which showed the old lion was wounded and could be replaced. But most importantly, he had made inroads into the minds of parliamentarians. The road for Jagee would no longer be a smooth one.

In a few days, Paul and company were thrown out of the Finance Ministry as well as the Sandwich Party, and obviously they moved into the Ball and Socket Party office. The romance between Paul and Colleen was growing in leaps and bounds. Perhaps more leaps than bounds. We will return to that part of the story later, once I find a writer who is an expert in romance to write that particular piece. This should happen by page 89. But whether it does or doesn't, we shall know definitely by page 93 and that's a guarantee.

Let's now return to the leader of the opposition, who had realized the enormity of his challenge, and the gravity of consequences that would result. He thus was presently spending 75 percent of his precious time in the lavatory.

Machado's mind had clearly flipped a switch. He now liked to communicate in a unique way, with sounds made up of only vowels, like 'eau' or 'eaa' 'eauee'. He also liked to blow air into one cheek at a time, and make clicking sounds with bubbles thus produced. Sometimes he would think he'd become a monkey and climb furniture. Other times he'd think he'd become a banana and assume a J position with his body. Of course, these acts didn't stop him from doing his duties as leader of the opposition in parliament. Colleen had him tied to his chair, and would hand him a Rubik's cube, which he would alternately try to solve and then eat. Now Paul and his cronies couldn't just start a revolution in parliament. Besides, overnight they had gone from the ruling party to the opposition. Realizing that Machado needed to be prepped up, Ray Chow and Amama were kept close at hand on either side of Machado's chair. Chow would hold the leash that kept him fastened to his chair and Amama would play mouthpiece. This he did by pretending to translate any and all of Machado's primate sounds. Machado soon got used to being fastened in a chair thus, especially once he had ceased to try and become a seated human banana.

Machado or no Machado, the parliament had become a volatile hunting ground with lot of axes to grind, lots of mud to fling, and lots more would soon hit the fan. Col. Jagee had clear battle lines. First up, the economy was in tatters because of poor leadership from the finance ministry. Who ran this ministry? Paul Huskee. Secondly, it's so easy to stay out when the kitchen gets too hot, so defecting to the opposition gives you an imprint of the character of Paul Huskee, a man who, once saddled with responsibility, dealt with it by taking a dive!!

Ray Chow quickly pointed out that since Paul Huskee's appointment was done by Col. Jagee himself, it was the President who was responsible for this mess. The Prez's rebuttal to this was to have a seven-minute coughing fit, after which (having bought sufficient thinking time) he explained that he had offered Paul a job in deference to his grandfather who had recently fallen out of the window. To this, Chow countered that the financial rot in the system had started five years ago when Jay Huskee himself was in charge of finance. Once again, an appointment the President was responsible for. An incensed Col. Jagee said that by this logic, he was responsible for everything, including the First World War. Chow replied that he had no proof about Jagee causing the First World War, but World War ll was a different story. Too long had Hitler, Mussolini, and to a lesser extent Hirohito have to carry 'that' cross.

Aghast that their leader was being compared to Hitler, as everyone knew that Col. Jagee was a full three inches taller, Jagee's supporters joined the debate. This they did by hurling paperweights at Machado, Amama, and Ray Chow. Chow and Amama decided to answer back in a far more mature way, i.e. by throwing all stationary that had jagged edges and points on them, such as pens, dividers, and compasses. Machado, sensing too much tension in the room, dealt with the issue in his own way by trying to touch his nose with his tongue, and occasionally succeeding.

I think it's only fair to say we have now reached

a point where, dear reader, you have done the hard yards, you have been through both frying pan and the fire, thereby proving your mettle and your worth. This most definitely earns you the right to join the story at its real beginning, to join the battle in earnest, so to speak. But before that, those of you who have started reading from this particular page, for those of you who have lost the first part of this book, and for those of you suffering from Parkinson's, or any related disease, let me outline our present situation. Paul Huskee, half lured by love, and half by disgust towards Col. Jagee, has defected towards the Ball and Socket Party. Jagee will now do all he can do to fix Paul Huskee and his cronies. Paul Huskee now sees Col. Jagee as enemy number one, responsible for all evils plaguing society, including both the World Wars, dengue fever, gangster war, and the unnecessary implementation of service tax.

Jagee must be brought down and defeated in the next general election, but to do that his reputation should be thoroughly besmeared, and his support, power, and influence eroded. Whilst in the Ball and Socket 'war' room, plans are afoot. Col. Jagee was putting together a dossier that would destroy Paul Huskee.

Jagee's words to his advisors were fairly clear, 'Bring me everything on Paul Huskee.' 'Everything' here is a concise version of that document on Paul Huskee.

'Paul Huskee is a male Libran, born on October 7th into an influential Gyaandostaan's political family in which all male members are known to shave. Inclined towards sports, his business acumen allowed him to come up with a few proposals for his grandfather Jay Huskee. This included an idea for a single seat belt in motor cars, that could be used on all four occupants of the car. Another idea was that of a liquidized version of ice, an invention which he was later told may have already existed. Then there was the scheme to transmit electronic currents to employee's shoes, thus allowing the employer to give them a mild shock, from time to time, to prevent any slackening on the job. To each of his schemes, his encouraging grandfather greeted him with derisive laughter and wild gesticulations. The type that sends a message that the person in question is completely stark raving mad, and should be simultaneously medicated and committed immediately.'

There were other less emphatic observations, such as 'Paul liked to wear socks while sleeping, and that the socks always had pictures of playful baby elephants on them. He also liked to sleep on his left side. Except at the time, he would be sleeping on his right side. Paul had or has little knowledge of politics, even less social and civic awareness, and is not known to be particularly charitable. He once gave a beggar the remains of his ice-cream cone, then changed his mind and took it back before the poor beggar knew what hit him. There is a chance that his grandfather's strange disappearance through an open window may not entirely have nothing to do with him!!'

This last sentence got Col. Jagee's juices flowing. He needed something to bring down the whippersnapper. And since he controlled the law, and the investigative agencies, these would be the right machinery to use against Paul Huskee. After all, that was the very nature of a democratic government. One in which the president could use official means to settle personal scores through untrue, unsubstantiated accusations.

Col. Jagee returned to bed that night very pleased with himself. Meanwhile in the 'war' room, the Ball and Socket think tank weren't exactly idle, except for Mr Machado who had now spent more time in the lavatory than any respectable plumber would in his lifetime. But we'll come to their counter plotting a little later because the next day, the President of Gyaandostaan had a very peculiar visitor.

6

Mr Bosh had done his schooling in Boston. He had a fluid New England accent and it left a very lasting impression. This was not because of his educational qualifications or his remarkable personality. This was because of his most peculiar name. His name was Bosh, Gomango Bosh. He was the chief public prosecutor in Bey, Gyaandostaan. Gomango Bosh was tall and thin, with shoulder length hair, not typical of the species of public prosecutor as seen worldwide. He had been summoned by the President who was presently jogging on his treadmill, backwards.

The President had on his shoes and his Saddam Hussein visage and not much else. Gomango Bosh preferred to retain his gaze on the President's shoes.

'Gomango, have you done it? D'you find anything?' asked the President in a genuine middle–eastern drawl which seemed to be his thing for the day.

'Yup, Mr President. To be fair, Mr Paul Huskee has paid all his taxes and has been an outstanding citizen,' Mr Bosh exclaimed.

Prez: 'I hope that's not what you've come here to tell me. Remember public prosecutors who are dismissed in the middle of their term don't find work that easily. Mr Crenshaw, for instance, is a parking attendant.

GB: 'I'm aware of that, Sir. I just handed him my car. Allow me to finish please. There is one tax however that's escaped deduction. It's an old archaic tax called the parliamentarian's tax, meant to be paid by parliamentarians. I did the math, and from Jay Huskee's term, for the past 29½ years, the Huskees owe, if you account for inflation and compound interest, 16 crore Ragoos.'

Prez: 'Are you sure?'

At this point, President Jagee was so excited that he stopped running for a couple of seconds, causing him to get swallowed up by the treadmill and finally land in a heap on the floor. One of his minders fetched his bathrobe, which for some reason had the words SPERM WHALE embroidered on it. President Jagee sat himself down and continued.

Prez: 'That is wonderful news. 16 crore Ragoos, that'll bury the traitor alive.'

GB: 'There is one small issue though.'

Prez: 'I don't care, just hang that bastard for this... this...er...beautiful parliamentarian's tax. Whose brainchild was it anyway? We should declare a national holiday after the founder of this tax.'

GB: 'It was the brain child of Jay Huskee on his first go as Finance Minister under the auspices of your father who was in a state of coma at the time.'

Prez: 'Oh, so maybe a national holiday will be too much. We've got too many anyway, 33 on the last count. How about a statue? We need statues. We can do with another statue. Yup, I think we'll give him 2 statues. After all the poor man fell out of a window... which is not so uncommon an occurrence as people think.'

GB: 'Sir, but please hear me out...'

Prez: 'Don't tell me we can't afford a statue, for God's sake. It could just be a bust, you know a little head, a little shoulder...'

GB: 'Sir, the problem is the entire parliament has not paid this parliamentarian's tax.'

Prez: 'No one, not one...okay let's keep the statue on hold for a little while, shall we?'

GB: 'Not a single parliamentarian in the past or present has paid even a Ragoo of this parliamentarian tax. So if we take action against Paul Huskee and his family, we'd have to take action against all parliamentarians. Every single last one of them.'

Prez: 'Now wait a minute Gomango, my fine young man, you may have got something there. Wait just a goddamn minute. Let's punish the whole lot.'

GB: 'The whole lot won't be able to afford the accumulated back taxes. We have to toss your entire parliament into jail.'

Prez: 'Best news I've heard in thirty years. No need for any statue. Let's jail the lot. I'll declare a state of emergency and go on holiday, just like dad did in '79.'

GB: 'But Sir, most of the MPs are from your party, they are loyal to your work for you, and if I may be so bold, earn a line of "credit" for you. Their 2+2 is your 4, if you know what I mean.'

Prez: 'You see Gomango, there is a difference between a Napolean, i.e. me, and a Gomango, i.e. you. You see a problem whereas I see a fantastic situation which will allow me to save this country that I love from incompetent untrustworthy buffoons like Paul Huskee and his crew. I say jail them all, for life if possible. It's a win–win situation. If they pay, good for our economy; if they don't, there will be one less moron to deal with. I could declare a state of emergency and run this state of Gyaandostaan in the democratic and egalitarian spirit of my ancestor Alexander the Great of whom you know I am a direct descendent...from his...er...mother's side.'

Colonel Jagee, on uttering the words Alexander the Great, slipped out of his bathrobe, puffed out his chest like a giant magpie, and started waving to an imaginary crowd in earnest. An effort more Caesar-like than Alexander, although, truth be told, one has never got to observe either.

GB: 'Oh, but there is one more thing sir, if I may be allowed to complete?'

Prez: 'What is it man? Can't you see how busy I am?'

At this point Col. Jagee had raised both his hands like a victorious heavyweight boxer, his ears were ringing with the cheers from an imaginary crowd.

GB: 'Sir, there is this small matter...'

Prez: 'Hurry up man...'

GB: 'You'd also be eligible...'

Prez: 'What? How dare you? What?!!!'

GB: 'You'd also owe, after 34 years in office, close to 200 crore Ragoos in tax. Plus, as President, the number has to be magnified tenfold according to the law. So we are looking at 200 crore Ragoos.'

Prez: 'Who came up with this "magnified" nonsense? Which complete idiot? Who?'

GB: 'The former President, your father, just after coming out of coma and going in for severe liposuction. Shall I give the order for implementation and collection of the pending parliamentarian tax, sir?'

But Col. Jagee had quietly slipped his robe back on. Alexander, Caesar, and Saddam Hussein had left the building.

Paul Huskee decided they needed to think out of the box. In fact, out of the next couple of boxes. A brainstorming session was indeed the need of the hour. However, he wanted a different geography. He felt that this would facilitate lateral thinking. He'd have the meeting at sea. Luckily, Amama owned a small boat, an inheritance from an uncle who was a shipping magnate and consequently, the owner of four large ships none of which he bequeathed his nephew. He did bequeath (I've just been informed from reliable insiders that the word bequeathed is now extinct like the mammoth though the word mammoth itself is not extinct) Amama this small tub that could fit 7 people. 7½ if they all held their stomachs in. The boat was named after Amama's maternal grandmother who is said to have drowned while bathing in her bathtub many years ago. Her name was 'Vesuvius'. But remember, Vesuvius in Gyaandostaani had nothing to do with the ancient volcano, although Amama's grandfather was known to have said he'd have preferred a match with the volcano instead.

The moment Paul set foot on the Vesuvius, he declared it to be the dirtiest boat he'd ever stepped on.

The boat smelled of stale banana leaves, possibly because thousands of old banana leaves were cluttered all over the Vesuvius. It had three steps in the boat's centre which led to nowhere. And the engine room was a bigger misnomer. There was no room, and there was barely an engine. That was, in fact, what looked like a hybrid between a typewriter and a sewing machine, which was unsuccessfully covered by a blue plastic sheet. Though a lot of ideas were exchanged on the vessel, none could actually be heard. This was due to the wailing sound of four old women on board who later turned out to be the engine itself.

The Gyaandotsaani seas were a source of pride and joy. But that was about 1500 years ago. It is said the great Macedonian loved the pristine blue water so much that he insisted on having a swim. And it was on this swim that he discovered shrimp for the first time, although there was some confusion about a shrimp being first discovered in his loincloth. Today, the seas were a different story. Most of the shrimp had choked to death with pollution and those that were left had committed suicide, some more than once. Many would have happily preferred the loincloth. The waters were deep grey, with all the muck and debris gifted to the sea by urban Gyaandostaan. Human divers were known to change colour within twenty minutes of being in these waters. In some rare cases, they were even known to change gender. Though that may have something to do with a few irate shrimps. Paul Huskee nevertheless went on with the expedition. A change of scenery was a change of scenery and just because in this case there was no scenery at all, it didn't mean there wasn't a change. It was Shabbir Hoossein who set the ball rolling. This he did by vomiting first on Amama, then into the deep sea, and then on Amama again. Most thought of this as divine retribution. Punishment for Amama. He deserved punishment for getting them on the boat. Amama himself felt quite relieved.

The smell of the stale banana leaves had made the journey unbearable, more so for Shabbir Hoossein whose nasal cavity made him suffer 75 percent more olfactory damage than the next person. But by repeatedly vomiting, Shabbir Hoossein had ensured the trip was aborted within 17 minutes of leaving the shore. As the boat (Gyaandostaani maritime regulations regulate that we must call it a boat, even though it was more like a few broken wooden boards and rusty nails interspersed with banana leaves than a boat in the rudimentary sense), meandered back to shore, Shabbir Hoossein had a Eureka moment. Except that since he had a bucket on his head at that time, no one could share this moment with him. Then Bella Terrace ripped the bucket off his head, not in order to hear Hoossein out, but to do a little vomiting of her own. Hoossein spelt out the proposal. 'Let's hack Jagee's personal computer. We'll know what he's up to and can stay one step ahead of him. We just need a way to get into his space.'

Paul loved the idea. 'Great idea, but who will do the hacking, and besides, how do we get into his office undetected?'

Shabbir Hoossein had no answer. I mean he had an answer, as we'll find out later, but at that moment he was engaged in a pitched battle with Bella Terrace for control of the bucket. Bella Terrace won and Shabbir

Hoossein had no recourse but to make Amama his recipient once again.

The man who was selected to hack into the President's computer went by the name Shampoo. Shampoo was about 5 feet 9 inches tall, of medium build, and was known as a friend and junior associate of Mr D'Souza. Nobody knew his origins or if he had any other name.

All that people know was that he'd been around for many years, and served in some professional cum personal capacity at Mr D'Souza's office. Since he always smelt of shampoo, his name was well served. He was also a friend of Paul Huskee's younger brother Mohan.

Also, like Mohan, he was incredibly feminine. Shampoo wasn't just a little girlie, he was far, far, far out girlie—the far end of the girl spectrum. The girliest of all girls. He was brilliant with computers. You know the tribe. They use PCs like concert pianists use their pianos. These two qualities meant that Shampoo was meant for the job, even though he was caught off guard with the make-up and the costume that came with the job.

Paul Huskee and his coterie decided the best way into the President's office would be through the route of an interior decorator. Word had it that Col. Jagee was trying to redesign his office. Like most of Col. Jagee's projects, he would start and soon forget the idea which is, thank God, why he didn't have any children.

Shampoo was given an all access pass, easily arranged as links and influential phone calls was par the course in Gyaandostaan.

A day was chosen when Col. Jagee and his cronies had left the country, ostensibly on some 'official' business, but everyone knew that official actually meant 'massage therapy', Col. Jagee's favourite sport.

Getting into the office was extremely easy. No one even checked Shampoo's accreditation. This in spite of the fact that he was dressed in a tight fitting blouse and skirt. His well shampooed hair was well hidden under a brown-coloured ladies' wig.

Shampoo (let's call him 'her' here, for the purpose of this visit and to avoid unnecessary confusion) settled down on Col. Jagee's desk and even ordered a cheese toast and watermelon juice from the canteen, as she started to browse through the files. Like most world leaders, Shampoo had to sift through lots of adult erotica, before she found a file named Paul Huskee code named 'Open Window'. Shampoo was in the process of opening the file when the door was flung open, and who should enter? Col. Jagee looking highly anxious and impatient.

Shampoo put her hand on her heart realizing that it was actually a false breast. She then put her hand on her head. She felt she was taking her last breath on earth, but at least the head was hers.

'Ah, thank God you're finally here.'

Col. Jagee rushed to her and pulled Shampoo out of the chair, planting a kiss on her well-painted lips. If Shampoo thought she had died earlier, she really wished she would die now, and with immediate effect.

What followed was the most shocking moment of Shampoo's entire life. The President of Gyaandostaan removed all his clothes and lay with his face down on the sofa cum bed in front of the desk. 'What are you doing?' Shampoo said.

'Ah you're right, give me a second.' So saying, Gyaandostaan's most powerful man got up, starkers, locked the main door, pulled out a bottle of oil from behind the desk, starkers, drew the curtain, and pulled down the blind, starkers, and then proceeded to hand the bottle over to Shampoo. Then, still starkers, much to Shampoo's horror, Col. Jagee, President of Gyaandostaan, lay down on the sofa cum bed, starkers, but this time face up.

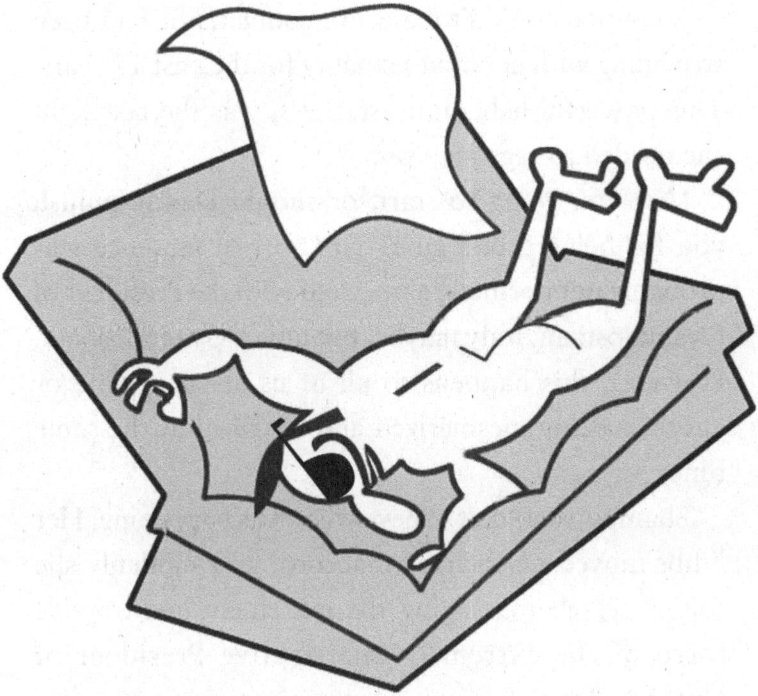

The President of Gyaandostaan removed all his clothes and lay with his face down on the sofa cum bed in front of the desk.

'Now love, the last time you were a bit rough, so let's have a gentler, smooth time of it today, okay?' said the Colonel.

Shampoo couldn't make eye contact. She had been struggling with her own sexuality for the past 17 years. This powerful behemoth, starkers, was the last sight she needed to register, ever.

'Are you going to start, or should Daddy punish you for being a bad girl?' This sort of sentence was probably not normally associated with the President of Gyaandostaan. Italy maybe, but not of Gyaandostaan. However, this happens to all of us at some time or another. Being mesmerized and horrified at the same time.

Shampoo couldn't believe what was happening. Her limbs moved on their own accord, and suddenly she found herself massaging the extremely unattractive torso of the extremely unattractive President of Gyaandostaan.

'Ah, that's better, remove my stress. Not everyone is lucky enough to get an opportunity to relieve the stress of the President of Gyaandostaan.'

Shampoo then did what all self-respecting men dressed as women, who were mistaken for masseurs, would do. She pulled hard at the President's chest hair.

The President winced, but seemed to like it. 'Again,' he insisted, like a child at a merry-go-round, 'again, again, again.' He went on, with each hair that was pulled out.

And then it happened, masseur and the massaged started talking. The President unlocked all his stress, which he told Shampoo was caused by that violent fool, Paul Huskee. He explained how he planned to bind Paul Huskee in some archaic parliamentary law and then he added, how if that couldn't be arranged, Paul Huskee would have to be taken out. To which the innocent Shampoo said, 'Taken out like a dog for a walk?'

At which point Col. Jagee repeated the line ' like a dog for a walk,' and then fell off the sofa cum bed in peals of laughter, starkers.

7

Let's leave Shampoo and Jagee's evil machinations aside and move to our love track, which for now isn't about Shampoo and Col. Jagee.

Colleen Connor and Paul Huskey had started growing fond of each other. On a scale of 1 to 100, Paul was roughly 77, in terms of 'madly in love'. Colleen was probably a more mature 1½ . However, working up close, Colleen started to notice lots of alluring things about Paul—the way he always wiped the chair with his shirt sleeve before sitting on it, the way the sweat from his forehead rolled down his cheeks and into his mouth, the way he shut his eyes and pretended to be asleep, while Mr D' Souza was speaking, until of course he really was asleep, and the way he swallowed beverages. He used to gargle with each sip for about 4–7 seconds before swallowing the liquid forcefully, making a bubbly sound. One that Colleen started to refer as a reverse burp. Now, when you start recalling an individual's burp fondly (even though a reverse burp is not really a full-fledged burp, but definitely owes some sort of allegiance to the burp family. Let's put it this way—in the reverse burp case, at least one parent was a conventional burp), then definitely, without any doubt, you are getting soft on the individual in question.

The couple was of course mostly surrounded by henchman and supporters. So, the initial romance was in crowded rooms. Crowded rooms have their own rules and dynamics for romance. Holding a gaze, passing stationery, and stepping on toes.

Stepping on toes may sound like a village in England, but has its own origin in nearby Flanders, where it went by the name 'footsies'.

In Flanders, during the town dances, men and women were lined up at opposite ends, like prisoners about to be shot. Obviously, many would have preferred being shot to dancing. During the event, the male would choose his partner by standing on the foot of the girl he desired. He then pushed down with all his might. If she could take on his weight, they danced. If on the other hand she squealed in pain, he'd stand on her other foot just to 'make a point'. Paul and Colleen found that footsie, on a crowded table, was as a contact sport, hard to beat. Of course, like all contact sports it came with its own set of challenges.

The first time they played, the sequence went like this: Paul's left foot on Colleen's right one led to Colleen's left foot on Paul's right one. This led to Paul's left foot on Ray Chow's left one. So Ray Chow's right foot landed between Amama's right and left ones. Amama's angry right one grazed Shabbir Hoossein's upper thigh and Shabbir's right foot made a beeline for Amama's groin. Ray Chow's knee smacked D'Souza's knee, and soon everybody started kicking Shampoo, including Colleen and Paul.

But with practice, the ancient sport from Flanders was mastered, and soon not just Paul and Colleen, but Paul, Colleen, Amama, Ray Chow, and Shampoo all became complete masters at it. But none of this prepared Paul Huskee for his first dinner date with Colleen Connor.

Now bear in mind that months had passed since Colleen Connor had met Paul Huskee and changed the political face of Gyaandostaan. Col. Jagee was plotting and clashing with Huskee and company on a regular basis. The Sandwich Party and Machado's Ball and Socket Party were on opposite sides of the political spectrum. And while all of this was going on, the country's leading newspaper *The Waving Flag* had requested Paul and Colleen for an interview together.

But, first a word about *The Waving Flag*—the word being 'fraudulent'. *The Waving Flag* was owned and run by Col. Jagee's family. Set up by his grandfather, it was initially named after his grandmother and called *The Seema*. This was during a phase when grandfather Jagee was madly in love with grandmother Jagee and in his blind devotion, tended to call everything after his beloved.

Col. Jagee's two aunts were called Seema. Of course, people felt he was taking it too far when Col. Jagee's dad was also renamed Seema. Soon after, 3 public parks, 7 roads, 5 national awards, as well as the national bird—a Pelican—were all renamed Seema. Some say Col. Jagee's father never recovered from this change, although there is enough proof that the Pelican did.

When Col. Jagee came to power, he rectified this, and changed the name to '*The Waving Flag*'. He wanted to call it *The Jagee* initially, but was convinced otherwise when every single employee quit on the spot.

The Waving Flag now acted like all newspapers should. It had three rules. Col. Jagee had to be mentioned 22 times at least, and in the Sunday edition 24 times, and also that his quadruple chin should be halved in photoshop before appearing in the newspaper. Besides, no one was to be shown bigger or taller than the President in any picture, not even if it was an animal.

The Waving Flag was constantly taking digs at Paul Huskee's gang. So this interview was looked upon as a peace offering of course. Paul Huskee took out a little insurance. He was videotaping the whole thing, and would be feeding it to the rival newspaper *The Glasnost Times*.

This paper was run by a Russian immigrant called Andrei. (For some reason all Russian immigrants were called Andrei in those days; these days they are all called Vladimir.) Andrei was a big fan of Mikhail Gorbachev, and he tried to honour his hero as well as the free world by naming the paper after a word which made Gorbachev famous. This initially confused his publishers who were adamant that *Times* was an English word. Truth be sought, nothing was known about Andrei. Where did he come from? Who were his friends? His profession? Hell, no one had even seen him speak Russian.

Although a much smaller paper, Andrei made sure he kept the dream of free speech alive, and obviously tended to side with Paul Huskee and gang.

The interview was set in a fancy restaurant called 'The Wild Bore'. Thus Colleen and Paul were finally on a dinner date together, though not really alone. About 7 photographers, PR persons, 3 managers, and 8 staff members were on hand. Paul was most surprised to see his interviewer—Col. Jagee himself.

When Col. Jagee entered The Wild Bore, the mood of the room got real sombre. All the staff jumped to attention as he had his early Mussolini face on. This is the one he used when he was completely devoid of humour, as opposed to just devoid of humour. People started running helter skelter, trying to look busy. It's a great gift to bring negative tension into a room. Col. Jagee had this gift.

Jagee sat down on the vacant third chair and started removing his shoes, then his socks. Then, as an afterthought, he put his shoes and socks back on, not in that order. All this time, he didn't offer any formal greetings to the other two. Since the conversation was recorded, I can swear on 75 percent of my ancestors that what you are about to read is true word for word. A copy of the interview is available in the Bey Central library. So when you're in Gyaandostaan, you can check it out for yourself. In fact it would be fairly accurate to say that close to 40 percent of all events in this book may have actually or may not have actually happened. Col. Jagee was caught a little off guard when Colleen spoke first. Her tone was rabid and judgemental. Two fine qualities.

C: 'Fired your journalist because he didn't mention you 74 times in his last column, Mr Jagee?'

Col. Jagee hated being called Mr Jagee. After all, he had gone through hell to get his title without really serving the forces, so much so that sometimes he wondered whether it would have been better to have just joined the army.

J: 'As usual your facts are as wrong as you yourself are. Let me correct you, its 22 times and no one has been fired yet, pending inquiry.' Col. Jagee said this with the air of a man who'd never heard of the word democracy. Although he secretly made a note to himself that 94 times seemed a better number.

P: 'Yes, but Colonel, why did you remove your shoes and socks and then put them back again?'

J: 'I don't know about her country, but in our country it's called "airing your feet".'

Jagee delivered the line like a stand-up comedian delivering a punch, and was taken aback by the lack of laughs in the room.

Jagee made a second mental note to himself. *Must get personnel to follow me around as hired laughing tracks.* His broad smile to himself was cut short by cryptic Colleen Connor.

C: 'It's a lot better than airing his views.'

It was the first legal, lethal punch and it landed fast and hard on Jagee's crusty visage.

P: 'Her country? She's more Gyaandostaani than you or me.'

C: 'To be honest I can't think of any country that'll actually have him.'

J: 'Now watch your mouth, don't you have any decency when speaking to a head of state?'

C: 'No. Don't you have any decency in still being a head of state?'

J: ' No...er...I mean yes. I mean er...you know what I mean.'

C: 'Paul, d'you know what he means?'

P: 'No, do you?'

C: 'No, bet you, even he doesn't know. Mr Jagee, do you know what you mean?'

But by now she was talking to an empty chair, as Col. Jagee, head of state of Gyaandostaan, had walked out of his own interview in a huff. His last mental note was to cancel the human laughter track.

And that's how Paul Huskee and Colleen Connor finally got their very own special dinner date, and what a euphoric mood they were in!

It was a huge moral victory. Mussolini had baulked; Italy may soon be theirs.

Once the newspersons and the hangers-on had cleared Colleen and Paul went to town, they drank everything on the menu card. Thrice.

Paul, of course, was waiting for Colleen to be quite inebriated before making his move. But soon, Paul was falling way behind. The Alcolympics were declared open when Colleen suggested they fall on the floor, assume the push-up position, and alternate sit-ups and push-ups. This was done by placing the drink under one's chin, whilst attempting the push up. Colleen worked up a furious pace. Paul, whose last push-up was 4½ years ago, had trouble keeping up. Irish drinking manners would soon triumph over Gyaandostaani ones. And keep in mind Gyaandostaani drinking customs were handed down by one of the great drunkards of history, Alexander the Great.

Next was the dancing. Colleen kicked her shoes off and asked Paul to join her by doing Arab springs across the room.

Sadly, Paul was not used to dancing on the table. Then Colleen insisted on the one-legged dance. In this old European art form, you dance on one leg whilst your partner holds your other leg. Soon, both partners are holding each other's legs, and though movement is limited, it can look quite pleasing to the eye, especially if the dancers are crabs.

In all this, Paul, ever the professional, kept telling himself, 'Make thy move, make thy move'. Paul found that as he got more drunk, he tended to use more archaic prose. In fact, to be totally fair to Paul, he was about to make his first move, when Colleen raised his right leg, which was trapped between her left leg and left hip, about seven inches more than bodily possible for any one life form barring amoeba.

It was Paul's first attempt at the Fosbury Flop, and one can say that in most certain terms that he hadn't quite mastered it. As he lay on the floor, eyes fixed on the ceiling, all he could tell himself was, 'Make thy move, make thy move'. Since the couple was now quite clearly the centre of attention, restaurant patrons, and staff gathered around them, egging them on. It was a

Then Colleen insisted on the one-legged dance.

moot point in Gyaandostaan that whenever the rich and famous wanted to have a good time, nothing was too much, nothing morally reprehensible or beyond the pale. For the ordinary Gyaandostaani, it was a different story.

Then it happened. As the crowd formed a horse shoe around the sanguine Paul Huskee, he himself did nothing to encourage the slow hand clapping. Soon he sort of realized it wasn't for him. Colleen descended from the table and took a predatorial gait, like a lioness, slowly but powerfully marking her run-up. She flung herself on the prone Paul Huskee. Their eyes met, as her heaving bosom lay on his confused chest. Paul kept on rambling incoherently about his 'move'. Then both came to that magical point where proximity tests romance. It's when you're so close that you either lock lips or break away awkwardly. Colleen pursed her lips, Paul closed his eyes and then he screamed. Colleen was off him and laughing. The audience that had gathered about was hysterical with glee.

Paul continued screaming as Colleen had landed on him. She reached behind his head and put a whole lot of ice cubes down his back. Paul slithered like a drunken snake, making the most effete of sounds, until some well-meaning staffer helped rid him of his cubes, although perhaps a bit too enthusiastically for someone of the same gender.

Colleen helped him to his feet, and then immediately challenged him to a game of strip-shots. If you finish your shot second, you remove a piece of clothing. Strong-willed as he was, Paul kept telling himself, 'Make thy move, make thy move'. He knew he had it in him to 'seal the deal'. And he did seal the deal, if by 'seal the deal' you mean lying naked in your own vomit on a restaurant floor at four in the morning in front of seven of the finest photographers in the country.

8

Col. Jagee kept pacing the floor of his office. This by itself was not odd, but for his insistence of having Shampoo in the room at the time. He had got increasingly fond of Shampoo and felt a level of comfort that he didn't feel with anyone else. Hence, pacing up and down in his office wearing only his socks was the ultimate signal to Shampoo that according to Col. Jagee, Shampoo was 'cool'. And it's not like he asked Shampoo to join him. Amazingly it wasn't like a sex ad. Shampoo, as for him, was like part of the furniture. Furniture that he could finally trust. As a leader who was being challenged, he had started becoming highly suspicious. He was very worried about coups and assassinations. Every new room he went to, he'd shut the windows and close the curtains, then find a corner from where he could face the entire room and stick to it. In spite of all this, his proposition to Shampoo came as a shock to all and sundry. So since Shampoo was aware of the proposition, for you and I, dear reader, are shocked that everybody was shocked.

'Shampoo, how would you like to be my food taster?' the Colonel queried.

Now keep in mind that Shampoo got his fair share of propositions of the same sex. But never in the history of propositions had a naked head of state, save the socks, propositioned him to be his food taster. (By the way, Shampoo has requested that we refer to him by the male gender until such a time when he feels comfortable switching publicly to the female gender. Our publisher, whose best friend is a cross dresser, feels we must honour the same.)

It was preposterous, out of the question, a disastrous idea, and frankly quite demeaning. So naturally, Shampoo said 'yes'.

Then Col. Jagee had an even better idea. 'Why don't I appoint you as my cook cum food taster?'

Shampoo nearly felt his feet buckle under him, which was quite strange as he was sitting at the time. This was even more ludicrous than Jagee's last suggestion.

Shampoo remembered he had only stepped foot in a kitchen three times in his entire life. On two of those occasions, he was trying to find the bathroom, so naturally he said 'yes' again.

'Good, great, we'll talk monies later, but obviously you don't have to worry about the food.' The funny thing is Col. Jagee did not mean it as a joke.

'Now Shampoo I want to talk to you about something very important.' With this Col. Jagee came and sat beside Shampoo and placing his hand on Shampoo's thigh, carried on. 'Should I wax my torso, Shampoo?'

Shampoo was now not at his most comfortable. Neither would you have been, if you had a 320-pound head of state sitting beside you, hand on your thigh, in the partial 'nude'. Shampoo was now mostly outraged and enraged. More outraged with huge dollops of enraged attached to it. So, naturally he answered 'yes.'

As Col. Jagee continued speaking, he started kneading Shampoo's ample thigh like dough. Shampoo remained transfixed like a rabbit who had been drugged first being skinned alive.

'That's what I thought. I'm a big fan of Aerodynamics, and body hair definitely slows you down. I read an article which says upto 1.5 percent increase in efficiency is noticed in a bare torso. Okay Shampoo (at which point the squeeze became harder), I've got an idea to bring down Paul Huskee and gang. It centres around Paul Huskee and my niece Bella Terrace.

Shampoo, who at this point felt he would be the first person to have died of thigh squeeze in medical history, suddenly woke up from his pain, and was suddenly all ears. Er…and a little thigh. The Col. went on.

'Bella Terrace's mother Bella Terrace Sr. is my younger sister.' It's what he said next flummoxed Shampoo. 'That makes Bella Terrace my niece.' It was now that the penny dropped. Shampoo realized the Colonel, General of the obvious, Field Marshall of the extra unnecessary information, and Great Dictator of 'Boring Conversationville' was actually only talking aloud to himself. Shampoo and everything else was quite redundant. Shampoo might as well as really have been furniture.

'Look, my niece and my sister own around 15 percent of stock in one of my companies. The company is called Raison d'être as they export raisins to Cuppe. Last week, I heard they plan to off load most of their shares. In a couple of weeks, I'm getting a law passed that will tax the export of perishable goods by up to 50 percent. The share price of Raison d'être will crash, and we'll have the two Bellas arrested for sort of insider trading and leaking privileged information. One by one we'll knock off Huskee's cronies, and then we'll eliminate that parasite Paul Huskee as well.'

Shampoo reacted to this diatribe in the appropriate way. He screamed, but that may have had something to do with his thighs being squeezed now with Col. Jagee's massive hands. The leader of Gyaandostaan, naked save for socks, didn't hear any scream of course. We have long since established that to him Shampoo was simply an extension of his furniture. Furniture, mind you, that he could trust, and occasionally squeeze. Keep in mind, dear reader, that in actuality Col. Jagee was not a very sexual person. His ambiguity will be explained in great detail in Book 3 of this series which, thank God, won't be out till 2027.

Ray Chow had no idea that he was walking down corridor 3 Junction Street in Bey's downtown area with Mr D'Souza. Mr D'Souza was of course sprouting forth in his incomprehensible style. Chow, as usual, pretended to understand by nodding wisely every 5½ seconds. Chow should have seen it coming, considering he had twice banged into a street light, while focusing on not listening to D'Souza. To be fair, as they crossed the road, D'Souza did warn him. Let's replay the conversation. First from D'Souza's perspective:

D: 'Watch out!'

R: 'You shut your mouth. Ooooh...arghh...'

Now let's look at it from Ray chow's perspective:

D: 'Shut your mouth.'

R: 'You shut your mouth. Ooohh...arghh...'

The good news was that the car he saw approaching was a Plymouth, sky blue in colour, with a lovely velvety engine sound. The bad news was that it was the last thing Ray Chow saw as he landed on the Plymouth's dashboard. Mr D'Souza meanwhile had stepped back on to the pavement, so he got a good view of the driver. It appeared to be a ferret. But D'Souza remembered that ferrets were not indigenous to Gyaandostaan. Besides, no ferret in his living memory could drive, let alone drive a beastly Plymouth with a stick shaft. If it wasn't a ferret, it had to be Col. Jagee's right hand man who looked and behaved like a ferret. That evil ferret-like face that did all of Col. Jagees' dirty work. In fact, the more he thought about it, the more he was convinced. Yup definitely! It must have been a ferret.

Ray Chow rolled off the car as the ferret hit the

breaks and fell on the floor in front. Meanwhile, the ferret hit the accelerator (as ferrets often do in such situations, and as happened several times in this book, so it can clearly be no accident), the car rolled over Ray Chow, leaving him looking a lot less 'Rayish', and a lot more 'Chowish'.

Meanwhile, Mr Ferret raced on, but as he looked back to survey his handiwork, he crashed his plush Plymouth into a pole at the edge of the sidewalk. The impact flung him out of his car, on to the sidewalk, and he landed head first, four inches away from Mr D'Souza's feet. After getting a close look at Gulu, D'Souza was certain of his identity. He had been right all along, it was a ferret.

Moonshine was a strange name for a hospital. But since the Huskee family owned a majority share in the hospital, they named it after Sophia Huskee's favourite fragrance, 'Moonshine'. And although, generally speaking, the world over hospitals aren't named after perfumes, it wasn't entirely illegal. On the 7th floor of Moonshine hospital was the casualty department. The first four floors had been given to a mall, so casualty was a little further up than necessary. However no one really cribbed, because if you insist on checking in to a hospital called 'Moonshine', you must be prepared for any and every eventuality.

Room 707 had Ray Chow. Well, most parts of him. Room no. 708 had Gulu. Well, most parts of him!

When Paul Huskee entered room 707, he was shocked, not at Ray Chow's condition, but because the air conditioner hadn't been turned on. This had to be Mr D'Souza's fault as he was famous for turning off air conditioners. Without even enquiring about Chow, Paul snapped at D'Souza.

P: 'Turn the damn air con on!'

D: 'Your father's old.'

P: 'Just turn it on.'

D: 'I'm wearing pants.'

This as you can guess was Paul's understanding of it. Let's now get a hand on D'souza's version.

P: 'Turn the damn air con on.'

D: 'I'm rather cold.'

P: 'Just turn it on.'

D: 'I really er...can't.'

With this, Paul, realizing that he was dealing with a frail old man with health issues, decided to take the sensitive road. So he threw D'Souza out of the room, and asked him to wait in the freezing cold lobby outside.

But D'Souza needn't have worried, if anything went wrong, room 709 was vacant.

Now let's cut across to room 708. When Col. Jagee and entourage entered, they were greeted by a strange sight!

Gulu's injuries were so peculiar that he was in almost a full-body traction, but that wasn't the pleasant part. That was of course the fact that he was in a rigid locked position of a man looking for a penny under a dining table (which was odd as pennies weren't indigenous to GYAANDOSTAAN). His body was face down, his buttocks elevated, as four massive pillows were under his groin. Both arms were in traction and were elevated, to make him look like he was permanently waving. His neck was in a brace and his head had a round cartilage like thing over it. This made him look like a gigantic praying mantis, which was also an impossibility as praying mantis and other praying mantis (the plural is very controversial) were not native to Gyaandostaan either. Shampoo, who accompanied Col. Jagee along with four bodyguards, was appalled.

It was Shampoo who asked the doctor if Gulu could talk. The doctor replied, 'Of course he can, but he'd faint immediately if he tried.' Then the good doctor showed them x-rays of a praying mantis in various poses. Col. Jagee tried to show interest, but after his third loud yawn, the x-rays were put away. Let's cross back to room 707 where the air conditioner was finally taking effect.

Ray Chow's injuries weren't that bad. If Gulu scored a 77 percent on 100 for injuries occured, Ray's would be a lowly 45 percent. In fact, his were mainly to his right hip and knee, which meant in non-political terms that, Ray would be leaning to the left for the next few weeks.

Ray and Paul spent the next few minutes chit-chatting. Paul did more of the chatting, Ray satisfied himself by simply breathing. Suddenly the door was flung open, and a dramatic, over rehearsed shampoo entered. One look at the still figure of Ray and Shampoo broke down. He flung himself on Ray's body and bawled away. Shampoo cried about love, the death of goodness, how he wanted to go cycling with Ray, and how Ray once borrowed a pair of his gym shorts and never returned it. He swore he'd turn Ray's house up and down till he found the pair. It was a navy blue one with hundreds of Dalmatian puppies running across it. A last memory, a last testament to his chum Ray Chow.

Now to the actual authenticity of the attraction to Ray Chow, nothing can be ascertained as no documented footage exists of either of them wearing the Navy blue shorts with Dalmatians on it, in the other's presence. At this point, using all his reserve strength, the now left handed Ray Chow pushed Shampoo out off his chest and onto the cold hospital floor. Soon Shampoo was administered a pain killer and he quickly spilled the beanson how Col. Jagee planned to get to Paul by knocking off his man Fridays, starting with Bella Terrace and her mom, who would be better classified as woman Friday, to be sure, but he hoped they got the point. He then rushed out and back to Col. Jagee, as a 37-minute toilet break at 3 in the afternoon would be tough to explain. Then once more the door opened and after a final inquiry into his gym shorts (the Navy blue ones dotted with Dalmatian puppies) and satisfied that they would be well looked after, and not neglected, but most probably because the pressure of Paul's hand around his neck was quite great, once more Shampoo imperiously executed a scorching exit.

I think, dear reader, we are at a point when our plot will finally unravel and that too in a deep dramatic fashion. Going by the sample segment test results, I can safely predict that exactly two pages from now, you will put up your hand and say, okay the story really starts from here, and wasn't it worth the wait.

Col. Jagee was absolutely gobsmacked. After easily getting the export tax on perishable goods raised by 50 percent, he sent men from the tax department, often called taxmen, to check into the two Bella's financial dealings. They returned with three cups of tea and a summons against the president, Col. Jagee.

Apparently, not only had they not off loaded Raison d'être shares, but in fact they bought 8 percent more equity on the day the new tax law was passed, ostensibly on the advice of their much loved relative, the reigning king of Gyanndostaan, Col. Jagee. Having filed a counter complaint case of being misled and misguided financially, the court moved to stop Bella Terrace's senior's bellowing male baritone, accepted the complaint, and a summon was issued on what used to be the most powerful figure in the land.

Gobsmacked he was. After throwing out all his aides, barring Shampoo, Col. Jagee did what he always did when anxious—he removed his clothes, save for his socks, and insisted on talking to Shampoo.

CJ: ' You think someone informed them? But only you and Gulu knew about the plan.'

Then Col. Jagee froze as the realization dawned. He stared hard at Shampoo, got up to his full height, put both hands around Shampoo's shoulders, squeezed tight, and then said, 'Gulu, that traitor, he must have passed on the information to Ray Chow. That's when they had the accident, I should have remembered the famous saying, "Never trust a ferret". It had to be him, in fact the last couple of times I asked him to have lunch with us he declined. Imagine being betrayed by a man who has seen me naked for the last 23 years, sometimes exclusively.'

At this Shampoo winced a little. To be honest he let out a cry, a small 'oooo', the one you'd make if you put icy cold water on, instead while expecting the hot. This had happened several times to Shampoo in the past, so he had perfected the 'oooo' sound. Basically his lips paused and the sound emerged for a full three seconds, after which he'd sneeze and clap his hands over his head.

Shampoo didn't want to drown the man. So he was most surprised when his own mouth without prior permission said:

S: 'Col. Jagee you're spot on. It has to be Gulu. I

myself have been noticing his strange behaviour over the last few days.'

CJ: 'Yes, like missing lunch, right?

S: Oh, lots of other stuff too, like using the toilet seven times a day, rubbing his back against a pillar in public, and last Tuesday I saw him put oil in the hair.'

CJ: 'Oil in the hair? Yes, that's really peculiar. Who does that anymore?' (The Col. said this while covering the two oil bottles on his desk with his left palm.)

S: 'And it wasn't even his own hair.'

CJ: 'Then whose was it?'

S: ' It was yours, Sir.'

CJ: 'Yes, you are right. What a fool I've been. Oil in the hair, scratching his back, missing his lunch, peeing too much—they all are signs of a devious mind. What a scoundrel!'

S: 'As devious as a ferret, Col. Jagee.'

The Gyaandostaani's had a word for a traitor and it was 'traitor'. Just like the English word for traitor, it was in the singular. Their plural for traitor was to say traitor many times and point to all the accused simultaneously. Just to be sure, Col. Jagee ruffled his hair. It felt wet. But was it oil or water? He couldn't remember!

9

Col. Jagee had had quite enough. He asked Shampoo to call in crack political analysts. The SWIM brothers were called in. The SWIM brothers were the best known political analysts of Gyaandostaan. They were so good at what they did that other countries such as the US, Finland, Slovakia, Namibia, and India had all used them. And barring India, they had a very high and accurate success rate. In the US, they were felicitated in the White House. Although a diplomatic incident broke on their way out, where they were finally allowed to keep the ashtrays but had to return the chandeliers, and the brass door handles.

In Finland, they were given the Order of Merit and free cell phones. Though, once again, there was controversy. However, the grandmother of the current home minister decided to drop the charges in the end. In Namibia, they were allowed to keep the bull they stole, although the national carrier finally put its foot down when they requested the Bovine be allowed on board as hand baggage.

India was another cup of chai though. Here they got the prediction wrong, as one political ally switched sides at the last minute, causing an upheaval or a reversed result at the very last moment. The SWIM brothers who just wrote the acceptance speech for the leader of the main party were arrested promptly, and the party who hired them refused to clear their dues or bail them out as they were still in the process of bailing themselves out.

Finally, it was the ambassador from Slovakia who pleaded their case and got them back to Gyaandostaan. However, this came at a price—the bull, the ashtray, the cell phones, and their various club memberships were appropriated by the new Indian Govt.

A couple of months later, the new government fell and the one that hired them came back to power. Mysteriously, it was the party which lost power that now turned to the SWIM brothers. They promised to return the bull and the ashtray. But the deal fell through because all the cell phones were missing.

When they entered the room, the SWIM brothers made quite an impression. They always wore purple suits, with maroon shirts and yellow ties. Sometimes they wore pants as well. They carried cigars in their hands, but strangely never lit them. Every five minutes exactly, they'd exchange the cigars with one another.

They both had high pitched voices, but it became exceedingly clear that they were well matched. This was due to a unique gift. A gift they had which was unmatched on mother earth. They always, always spoke simultaneously.

When the SWIM brothers entered Col. Jagee's office, they were greeted by Shampoo, standing over a sleeping Col. Jagee. The Col. was lying face down on his desk, whilst Shampoo was oiling his back and giving him a massage.

As Col. Jagee started speaking, his head remained face down in the desk. He spoke for a few minutes on different things, the need of the hour, the right response, the unblemished record. Whether tweasers could remove fleas from humans? Then he asked them if they'd join his team, and as he did so, he looked up. He was a little threatened to see that the SWIM bros had removed all clothing and were now sitting next to Shampoo, in an apparent attempt to await their turn for a massage by Shampoo, the little fellow. Col.

When they entered the room, the SWIM brothers made quite an impression. They carried cigars in their hands, but strangely never lit them.

Jagee loved the idea, and flinging the towel off him, he jumped up and joined them around the settee.

There, in the President of Gyaandostaan's private office, on a clean black settee, the SWIM brothers and Col. Jagee discussed his political road ahead, and they did so absolutely in the nude. Though it must be said at the threat of causing unrest that the SWIM brothers had their cigars on them all the time.

The SWIM brothers had done their homework. Although this was a habit they inculcated in school, it was one they never slackened over the years.

They made a 10-point improvement proposal which they presented in a charming audio visual. Now since books are prehistoric forms of communication, I can't share the audio visual in all its specific finery here, but I'll try and recreate as much as I can, and retain as much as I can of the original so as to maintain the impact.

Slide ❶ - shows a quick fluid look at the evolution of man. First the preneanderthal, then the homosomething or another, then Col. Jagee, then Paul Huskee, and after a black cut out morphed version of col. Jagee and the preneanderthal man. Slide 1's voice over says: As man evolved, he reached his zenith in the form of Col. Jagee. Then this man (Paul Huskee) appeared, and Col. Jagee was reduced to this (final slide of resplendent Jagee/

preneandethal). As long as Paul Huskee is around, Col. Jagee will always look like a retarded species, a relic of the past, a forgotten specimen.

Slide ❷ - shows a bunch of bikini clad women running on the beach. VO: This slide has no significance, it's just for visual relief.

Slide ❸ - children are throwing stones and laughing at something. The camera pulls out and it's a picture of Col. Jagee. VO: Power and ridicule go hand in hand. Lose a little power, gain a little ridicule.

Slide ❹ - picture of two hand models. VO: This slide is for recreational purposes only. Hand models available for parties, functions, ad shoots etc. CALL 777 FUN WITH FINGERS, NOW.

Slide ❺ - shows two Gorrilas (silver backs) in the active art of mating. The action is intense. Suddenly both see something that disgusts them. They cover their eyes, break away from the act, and run helter skelter in a horrific terrified manner.

The object of their fear? The camera pulls wide to show a statue of Col.Jagee, right there in the jungle. VO: Public approval can wane fast. Then all markets desert you.

Slide ❻ - has a man/woman dressed as Col. Jagee. But in rags and the man/woman is crying. VO: When the pressure is on, wrong choices are made. Form can be fickle and you get bent out of shape.

Slide ❼ - GOLDEN CROWN HOLIDAY HOMES available at good prices. VO: Need a break, don't settle for less. You deserve Golden Crown, the resting place for the rich and famous. Then there is a montage of famous stars such as Clint Eastwood, Meryl Steep, Nelson Piquet, James Oliver, Ussain Bolt, Dan Brown etc. VO: These stars may or may not have stayed in Golden Crown. Now you make the right choice.

Slide ❽ - opens with a life size cut out of Col. Jagee with a large bucket hovering over his head. Next to the cut out stands a small panel. As people pass by, they press a red button on the panel. At this the bucket tips over, and empties what appeared to be bodily waste produce on the cut out's uncomplaining head. VO: A reputation lies in tatters. From king to dustbin, lying in a pool of garbage, waste personified. Mangled refuse. Dirt and grime personified.

Slide ❾ - opens with a picture of a morgue (here unfortunately the AV presentation ended due to a slight unforeseen incident). Even as the ninth slide came on, the SWIM brothers found themselves in a bit of bother. With ape-like agility (clearly inspired by slide no. 5), Col. Jagee had leapt at them and grabbed their windpipes, one in each furious hand. He was squeezing hard and screaming in Gyaandostaani. Sadly, all the words employed here can't be used. I will, however, translate the gist of his speech leaving blank spaces for those that can't be explained. ' Evil twins (blank), mother a mango seed (blank) (blank). Tie up your genitalia and (blank) to her (blank). Pull out the nose hair (blank) rectal passage (blank) (blank), and turn your pancreas into (blank) (blank) (blank) (blank) (blank) (blank).'

At this point, one SWIM brother seemed to lose consciousness; the other was in a far better position, as he was only vomiting ferociously, but in the right direction.

It took Shampoo 20 minutes to extricate the President of Gyaandostaan from the two SWIM brothers. Then another 17 minutes to extricate one SWIM brother from the other. To ensure better sense prevailed, alcohol was served. Then Shampoo convinced all three to do the right thing, so they all put on their clothes.

Then, standing behind the settee, making sure there were three pieces of furniture between them and their predator, the SWIM brothers outlined their plan. As they did, they signalled for helmets, which Shampoo provided in a jiffy. In a nutshell (or any such non porous container), the brothers explained how Paul Huskee's rise coincided with the Col.'s fall. Public opinion was eroding quickly. Popularity was plummeting since they didn't see a reversal of this in the near future. Because of Col. Jagee's rampant use of law machinery for furthering personal gain at the cost of the country's eco-socio health, the best thing to do was call for early elections, while the Paul Huskee wave hadn't yet become irresistible.

If the Prez. played to his strength (lying, deceit, treachery, and cunning), Paul Huskee could still be stopped in his track.

When they finished, the SWIM brothers had reached the back of the room, and were quivering like frogs on a laboratory table for beginners. They had no trace of physical courage in their entire DNA. In fact, they were famous for their panic attacks that were frequent and severe.

The SWIM brothers, having gained back the President's confidence, decided to switch to e-mail for further correspondence, following the time-honoured tradition of safety first.

This is the contents of the first one.

'Oh great benefactor, oh overlord of the oppressed masses , oh over exalted overseer of all Gyaandostaan. Oh, ( ) (the long blank was to allow Col. Jagee to fill in his own adjectives describing himself as the SWIM brothers were firm believers that Col. Jagee was the one who knew Col. Jagee the best. A fact that was greatly appreciated by Col. Jagee).

'Your popularity knows no bounds, great one. Yet, as a safety precaution, purely an extra totally unnecessary safeguard, in the impossible event that you may have lost one, maybe even 2 supporters, we deem it best for you, if you were to create a series of articles in that great free and fair press machine that you own totally: *The Waving Flag*. The articles could be penned by you (with a very teesny weensy little help from us, not really with words as you are at best at that oh overlearned one, but more with say punctuation, the odd comma, even maybe an extra full stop.)

'So can we aim for one article every single day for the next 2 days? Obviously the articles will be a signed by different people, none of whom is really you. Though in truth, all will be you, which would be fitting as Gyaandostaan is you, and you are Gyaandostaan, which of course is not a reflection of your size, but of your greatness.

'For the first article, we have chosen is a writer, a 19-year-old boy who doesn't exist, called Fleicher Ankol. We've put together, if we may, a few words, just a couple more punctuations, really, for your perusal. Peruse and add to our bleak inferior verse, your unbelievable over-talented literary skill, that wreaks havoc at Gyaandostaani literary festival every single year. As can be certified from the fact that you have won the 1st prize for the past 27 years, and for at least 5 of these years you hadn't even submitted a book. And on 7 occasions, you repeated the same book, *Divine Secrets of the Ya Ya sisterhood of Rebbecca Wells.* We have only one request, and that is since we are suffering from a viscous head cold, during the exercise in punctuation, we may have sneezed a bit from time to time. Sneezes as you know tend to scatter words, helter skelter, so amidst the commas and question marks, you may find a few extra words here and there crawling over the page; this is our humble contribution. As a man who nominated himself on past 19 occasions for the Booker Prize (the fact that you haven't won yet is one of the deep mysteries of the modern world along with the lochness monster, the abominable snowman, and the futile search for a replacement to ajinomoto in Chinese cuisine).

'I'm sure you'll be able to twist and turn our putrid outpourings and convert it to the best literary effort the world has ever seen, comparable to the Great Bard, Bernard Shaw, and Pico Iyer himself. Below is our miniscule contribution to next Tuesday's Front page:'

Dear Editor,

Call me Pleisher. I would like to sing a song for the greatest son of Gyaandostaan since Alexander. I would also like to sing a song for Alexander, but as any student of music knows, you can't sing two songs simultaneously. So I'll sing a song for today's hero, a man who defies description. A magnificent servant of Gyaandostaan who always puts his country before himself, especially when he travels abroad. How quickly we GYAANDOSTAANIS forget our heroes? Who talks of Shemen the significant, who walked around the entire world on one leg just to prove that two legs were one too many? Who remembers Pearl of Panglula who donated both her kidneys and then had them returned all in one week? Who really remembers Abbey the archtypical, who accidentally discovered a cure for ringworm disease, while trying to make the first vodka/wine hybrid?

We've failed all the great citizens, let's not fail today's greatest GYAANDOSTAANI (none bar none)—the President of GYAANDOSTAAN, Col. Jagee. I would begin by rating all his myriad achievements, but who has the time to listen? However, in the interest of being specific let me note down a few. Here are Col. Jagee's top 7 achievements.

1. *He has made changes in Gyaandostaan*
2. *He can box squat 300 pounds*
3. *He has issued decrees*
4. *He can box squat 360 pounds*
5. *He has made flossing mandatory for all citizens*
6. *He has opened many doors*
7. *On his own*

Let us not forget today's hero, like we have forsaken many others. Today when you go to work, remember Col. Jagee, your guardian and guide, because he hasn't forgotten you, you and you. (Note the 'you's continue for the next 3½ pages of the paper, and then get interrupted by the sports pages after which they continue down from page 7 into 11).

Col. Jagee liked what he saw, namely his name many times in print. He knew he had written an outstanding article, so to speak. After all his story must be told. News can't be silenced, and as the article proved, the people loved him. And it is a scientific fact that what we read in print, we tend to believe as Gospel. This in fact formed the basis for the success of many religions.

Bella Terrace was livid. 'I can't believe he's done this, gone and announced early elections.' Shabbir Hoossein wanted to rest, but since she was choking Ray Chow at the same time, better sense prevailed and Shabbir sent for a nurse. As the nurse medicated her, Bella continued, 'The trouble with all of you is you don't know how to look ahead. Politics is trickier than chess, you can't just rely on the Sicillian defence. This man is a cunning shrewd plotter. We've got to engineer something of our own. Early elections will work in his favour.

Ray Chow lying on the hospital bed tried to respond. But 700 sedatives had left their legacy, and all he could offer was a 'caw' much like a sophisticated crow who had studied elocution and electric literature at GU (Gyaandostaan University). Mr D'Souza dare not contribute, and Amama who was standing dangerously close to Bella Terrace looked at Paul Huskee for security.

Huskee moved Amama behind the hospital bed

and then spoke his piece. 'We've got Shampoo in place, we are getting information ahead of time and in any case I've drawn out a possible ways to get at him. We attack the flagrant flouting of rules by his company where we've got Machado to sign off on any or all transgressions. The Sandwich Party has a lot of explaining to do from unpaid parking tickets upwards. Shampoo says we can nail him on his vanity cum eccentricity. You see he likes to conduct high level meetings, business lunches, and senior cabinet meetings in the nude.'

Two weeks later, the election date was announced.

It was typically an awful day. Awful, as the American vice-president was in town. So as usual, when a visiting dignitary came to town, Bey was at a standstill. Roads were cleared, citizens had to take cover, the army and the police went out to disturb the peace and keep the roads free of Gyaandostaanis.

Pregnant women about to deliver were asked to come back the next day; trauma and terminal patients were asked to hang in there and not leave the house and bother the hospitals. Children were asked to go to and from their schools via another city. The vice-president was in town to sign a deal whereby Gyaandostaan would be given 16 surface inter continental ballistic missiles. In exchange, the vice-president would get a free lunch and a comfortable stay at the PONP HOTEL. (The four letters P.O.N.P. stood for the four pillars of Gyaandostaan, but no one could remember who the four pillars were.)

The Vice-President addressed the Parliament. He spoke of how he hoped to share America's three greatest inventions with the Gyaandostaan people. He noticed how the first two—chapstick and hot dogs—were already in Gyaandostaan, hence he felt it is as essential that IBM (Inter Continental Ballistic Missiles) follow suit.

He spoke about how chapstick had saved many marriages, how hot dogs had brought America and Canada together. Yet if they wanted to, they could remove Toronto and Edmonton from the map, in the same time as it would take time to eat a hot dog! Yet, probably a little longer than it would take to apply chapsticks.

Then he spoke of the greatness of Gyaandostaan. A place Alexander the Great mentioned three times on his death bed. His exact words, 'Oh God Gyaandostaan! For God's sake get me away from Gyaandostaan, please please don't take me back to that infernal Gyaandostaan', remaining etched in our collective memory forever.Then he turned his attention to Col. Jagee. A man who had spent two years in America. (For assaulting airline staff on an Air America flight, he was given a 3-year sentence, 1 year suspended for good behaviour.) How he was a model prisoner! No literally, how he modelled at all the prison fashion shows with great aplomb. It was in this period that Col. Jagee wrote his primary prose on penitentiary life. The book explained in detail how the American system of prison, with four non-veg meals a day, access to gymnasiums, libraries and recreational facilities, completely air-conditioned, meant that it was comparable to a 4-star hotel in GYAANDOSTAAN. He titled the book *My Struggle* but lost interest after 17 pages and started drawing pictures, mostly of himself. The book was never published.

Getting back to his modelling stint, he was so enthusiastic that he finally had to be handcuffed on the ramp itself, because of his propensity to remove all his clothes. He loved the ease with which Col. Jagee bought his twin doctorates from the University of Pennsylvania, located in Toledo. And yet, he never flaunted those degrees, preferring instead to go by the humble rank of colonel. A title he picked up during a company picnic weekend (7 years ago), and subsequently never returned. He said America's doors were always open to Gyaandostaani people, and although the one across the Rio Grande was temporarily out of order. He spoke of how he honeymooned with his third wife in Gyaandostaan for seven days, and enjoyed the first four. He also honeymooned with his second wife in Gyaandostaan , but didn't want to talk about it as he had forgotten to take her back. He then threatened to introduce Obamacare to Gyaandostaan. At this point Col. Jagee called for a ten-minute recess, which in typical Gyaandostaani style was held for 2 hours and 27 minutes. After the resumption, Col. Jagee spoke of how the vice-president had failed to humbly speak of his own accomplishments, which included, fighting in the Iraq war, appearing in a soap dish commercial as the soap dish, and avoiding Arnold Schwarzenegger at three consecutive cocktail parties, when the scandal broke. He then added, 'As a proud democracy, we encourage dissent, freedom of speech, expression, and the right to eat ice cream cones left handed. Even though our next general election is two years away, I'm throwing down an open challenge to my competitors to overthrow, if they may, my government. I have scheduled the elections for the next month Oct 24th and 25th. Also 27th, but not 26th, as that's the day I get my weekly massage and my masseurs overbooked till April, so I can't change my date. Let the opposition, with their barbs and taunts, now pick up the gauntlet. Let the people of Gyaandostaan know that I will triumph convincingly, because not only is God on my side, but more importantly so is America!! To which the seated American vice-president extended his left hand and shook it, like he had the early stages of Parkinson's, which strangely he did. It was the universal sign for comsee comsaa, or fifty fifty, or don't know for sure, or early signs of Parkinson's. As Jagee sat down, his supporters roared their approval; some threw their belts in the air, one of which landed on the vice-president. Mayhem ensued, as security men started whipping the Sandwich Party Members of Parliament, who fought back by pointing their fingers and running helter skelter. Col. Jagee surveyed the situation and knew there was only one thing to do. He invited the vice-president back to his office for a massage.

The SWIM brothers were sweating profusely. In fact they seemed to be sniffing, even crying. They found Colleen Connor even more intimidating than Col. Jagee. They both had one of their simultaneous thoughts, *What if she also liked to conduct interviews with her clothes off?* The sweating got worse.

It was Shampoo who at much risk to himself had got the SWIM brothers to visit Colleen. He knew they were intimidated nay rattled by the President. He knew this because every time he mentioned Col. Jagee, their voices got a little higher. However, as the conversation continued and Colleen didn't start disrupting, they felt a little more relaxed, and at one stage even stopped holding hands.

Colleen outlined her proposal which was that while they advised Col. Jagee, they were actually working for Paul Huskee and the Ball and Socket Party. They would be paid to make sure Col. Jagee who paid them to ensure he wins loses. That is they'd be paid twice, and whatever the result, their score would be 1 win, 1 loss, so 1 all.

The elder SWIM brother looked away in fear. He remembered how Paris Broskee mistook him for her brother, and held him by his heels over a dry swimming pool. He remembered how Paris laughed as she bounced his head 27 consecutive times on the swimming floor. He remembered how after the incident he thanked her and suggested they do it again sometime. He remembered how this resulted in another 27 bounces off the pool floor, in full public view of his entire family, friends, and three senior members of the police force.

He then replaces Paris Broskee with Col. Jagee, and the visual took a turn for the worse as Col. Jagee was naked during the entire operation. Also he wasn't going to stop at a mere 27 bounces.

He thought of the option of separating him and his brother, one to work with Col. Jagee and one with Paul Huskee, but that would be futile as they always did everything together, and it would be next to impossible for one to go to the toilet in one side of town while the other's trapped in a car on the other side. He thought of giving a medical certificate to get out of discharging their duties, but they realized that every time a doctor examined them in the past, he would insist on keeping them for weeks for further examination. This further examination led to a lot of probing with metal objects, which left them with no sensation below their knees.

Colleen sensed their anxiety and apprehension, especially after they asked for pain killers. She appealed to their sense of patriotism, but they told her in no uncertain terms that they were both numb, and had lost all sense of feeling, except at the back of their knuckles. They added that if Col. Jagee caught them in this web of deception, he may never put his clothes back on again. Then they shuddered and said, they heard he had a swimming pool at the basement of his building, and worse that it was most of the year…empty.

Colleen at this point lost her cool, and asked them curtly if they were interested or not. From under the office table, the SWIM brothers asked if they could e-mail their answer to her, once they put up three countries between her and them.

At this point, Shampoo picked up the phone and dialed Mrs SWIM, the mother of the brothers who was a staunch feminist and a supporter of Colleen Connor. The SWIM brothers were told to SWIM with the tide. The noose around Col. Jagee was closing.

10

Ray Chow decided to let bygones be bygones as he was being discharged. On the way out, he decided to visit Gulu. Do the magnanimous thing. Gulu looked like a squirrel in a hammock, covered in plaster, his eyes rarely visible. His treatment was going to take some time. Chow wanted to make his piece, so he went really close to Gulu and stuck his tongue out. Then he passed on the choicest Gyaandostaani abuses known to man. And just before leaving, he pulled at the only visible part of Gulu, his big toe on the right foot, and bent it backwards.

Back in the Ball and Socket premises, Ray Chow outlined his cunning plan. He had an uncle who was pretty senior in the Communist Party in China. He may not remember Ray, but 40,000 US dollars could improve that memory. Col. Jagee was very keen on increasing trade with China. But China didn't like Jagee since they had heard of his nudism. And more importantly, they felt that colonel was too low a rank to run a country; not the most communist of thoughts! If only Ray could ingratiate himself with the Chinese top brass...then get all the trade contacts exclusively for the Ball and Socket Party. It seemed far-fetched but was well worth a shot. Jagee would try and put a spanner in the work of course. But even he dare not go against the diktat for mighty China.

Ray had only one slight misgiving about his brilliant plan—he didn't know which one was his uncle?

Paul Huskee thought it was worth a shot. Amama and Mr D'Souza were deputed to go with Ray Chow. Amama was a good level head to go with Ray's brilliance and Mr D'Souza deserved a holiday. And since most of the conversation was through interpreters, maybe at least China would be able to figure out what Mr D'Souza had to say. Not to mention that good fortune may strike and he may remain in China. As it turns out, this wasn't that far from the truth. Although, as this may be a work of fiction, it's hard to really guess what is the truth... er...truth be told.

And of course there would be no compulsion to bring Mr D'Souza back.

Mr Jogen Baglooloo got up slowly, tears in his eyes. He decided that maybe he hadn't made himself clear enough, so he prostrated himself before Col. Jagee and begged him not to sack him. Col. Jagee, who was seated behind his desk wearing only a cushion, pressed a button. Two large bodyguards appeared who whisked the hysterical Jogen Baglooloo away while trying not to look at yet salute Col. Jagee at the same time. Col. Jagee lit a cigar and contemplated. The SWIM brothers told him to make some changes to show the public he meant business. On a professional level he did this by sacking his home minister Jogen Baglooloo. On a personal level, he did this by wearing socks to all future meetings. Jogen Baglooloo had been around since Jagee's birth. He was initially a car cleaner who graduated to being a driver, and then a foster father to Col. Jagee, as he would pick and drop him from all his engagements, help with his homework, braid his hair, get his pals over, not to mention laundry and dry-cleaning. Although the last was rarely an

Two large bodyguards appeared who whisked the hysterical Jogen Baglooloo away.

issue as the young Col. Jagee rarely wore any clothes. However, off late, Baglooloo had become old, hard of hearing, unresponsive, and largely comatose. Normally, these would have been ideal qualities for a cabinet minister, but Col. Jagee was now looking at the larger picture. Baglooloo was like family. If Col. Jagee was willing to remove Baglooloo for the greater good of Gyaandostaan, this would be a fantastic PR exercise for the now slightly beleaguered leader. Arguably also the only world leader who was a practicing nudist at the time. And just to show that he wasn't without a heart, Col. Jagee had planned to offer Jogen Baglooloo his old car cleaning job, once again.

He called for a meeting with his new home minister, Shampoo, and the SWIM brothers. According to the Gyaandostaan Constitution page 78, Article 2C, no wait...page 93, Article 11A, no page 296, Article 16E recurring, the Prime Minister may appoint up to 3 cabinet ministers who are not elected officials of parliament. Luckily, Col. Jagee had long since broken that rule as 27 of his 43 member cabinet ministers were non-elected officials. This list included his carpenter, 2 gym instructors, a pizza chain owner, and 3 members of the boy band 'GAGAGA', who were, along with GYAANDOSTAAN's roads and bridges, among the most hated and useless things in the entire country. Please note that GAGAGA were originally GAGAGOO but changed their name to GAGAGA after consulting a numerologist.

The SWIM brothers sat as far away from the Colonel as they possibly could. This he didn't notice, but he did find it odd that they both occupied the same chair. The new home minister Shampoo seemed quite unaffected by his own recent greatness, and it's he who steered the conversation towards the 'need' to do something for the ordinary people of Gyaandostaan. A thought that had never occurred to any previous Gyaandostaan leader, Col. Jagee included, in the last 200 years.

Shampoo: 'According to them (pointing at the terrified twosome), you have to appease or do something drastic for the greater good of the population.'

Col. Jagee: 'I've got it. Since we have parking of cars in odd numbers on Mon, Wed, and Fri and even numbers on Tue, Thurs, and Sat, why don't we switch? Let's change it to even numbers on Mon, Wed, Fri and odd numbers on Tues, Thurs, and Sat.'

Shampoo: 'That's one way to er...go. Fellows, any ideas?'

He aimed this question at the SWIM brothers who at the time, completely uncomfortable with the attention they were getting, were squirming more than swimming. Sheer panic was on their faces, and they were trying to push their chair further into the wall behind them, in the eventual hope that they'd disappear into the wall along with the chair. Shampoo saw the anxiety.

Shampoo: 'Let's look at what are the basic needs of our poorer sections? What are they lacking?'

Col. Jagee got so excited to answer the question that he stood up in a great hurry, and doing so deserted the cushion, a visual that caused the SWIM brothers to experience even greater levels of stress. But try as they might, the damned chair wouldn't go into the wall.

Col. Jagee: 'I know…I know…ooo…me, me.'

Shampoo: 'Go ahead Col.'

Col. Jagee: 'Massage parlours. My driver is always complaining about aches and pains, and the poor soul has no access to a massage parlour. We need to take massages to the people.' As he spoke, he seemed to be advancing toward the brothers SWIM. Shampoo quickly intercepted the Col. in an effort to stop the SWIM brothers from having what now looked like heavy seizures. This he did by placing the cushion between himself and the leader of Gyaandostaan.

Shampoo: 'Very good, Colonel. Spot on! But that

would mean us spending valuable state funds. Let's find something cheaper.'

Col. Jagee: 'Oh I love that word "cheaper". Now you're really thinking, Shampoo. I could kiss you!!'

Shampoo armed himself with another cushion only as a precautionary measure.

Shampoo: 'Yes cheaper, and easy to implement. What say we announce an end to all power cuts? No more power cuts on Mondays and Thursdays. Power for everybody forever.'

Col. Jagee: 'Well, it's clearly as not as good as my massage idea…'

Shampoo: 'We'll come to your massage idea later. Let's not spoil them. They'll love the "power" idea. We could call our campaign "Power to the People". It'll make you extremely popular. By giving them power, you are giving them "power". Did you get it, Sir?'

Col. Jagee's chest was blooming now he was warming to his greatness.

Col. Jagee: 'By giving them power, we are giving them power… Yes, what is it?'

Col. Jagee noticed one of the SWIM brothers appeared like he was trying to make a point. The other one of course appeared to have slipped into a comatose state.

Col. Jagee: 'What is it? Stop squirming like a jelly fish and speak up man!'

Shampoo went over to the chair in the wall and held the courageous SWIM brother, the one who hadn't yet passed away, by his hand.

SWIM brothers: 'But we, we...don't generate enough power to sustain such an effort. We may soon run out of power...unless...'

As usual when the speech started, it came from both the brothers simultaneously. The dead as well as the alive one.

Col. Jagee: 'Go on. Unless...unless what...'

SWIM brothers: 'Well, you could announce the power to the people, quickly hold elections, win on this popular wave, and then promptly triple the load shedding after coming back to power, to balance it all out.'

Col. Jagee let out a cry. A mournful lament initially which turned into a shrill cry very similar to the call of the wild heron when its courtship has been accepted by another heron or a young bull frog who sounds a lot like a heron.

Col. Jagee: 'Come here you two, give Daddy a hug. Brilliant, absolutely brilliant.'

As he advanced towards the SWIM brothers,

sans cushion, arms akimbo, the brothers collapsed. Shampoo did what he had to do. He tackled the President of Gyaandostaan, rugby style, just before he made contact with the SWIM brothers. And thank God he did that because if the leader of Gyaandostaan made minimal contact with the SWIM brothers, they would have been dead before they hit the ground.

However, Col. Jagee was ebullient, even ecstatic. His short-term thinking style was perfect for such a plan. He believed Tuesday was best planned on Monday without a care about Wednesday. Thus, Thursday was always disastrous, and frankly he never quite reached Friday. As Col. Jagee got up and headed to behind his desk, the SWIM brothers relaxed just an incy-wincy bit. They had learnt one of life's important lessons today i.e. wooden chairs, normally, just don't go through walls.

11

The best way to describe China was that it was, er, Chinese. A beautiful country which, like Gyaandostaan, had all kinds of different terrain, weather conditions, and climes.

However, we won't discuss China in detail. Not because this writer hasn't been to China, or hasn't bothered to research the geographical mass that is China, or is far too lazy to even Google China, just so that he could create a genuine Chinese canvas and landscape for the China excursion. No we won't discuss China because Gyaandostaani secret agents (agents who are so secretive that often they themselves don't know they are agents) investigate anyone who writes glowingly about China or glorifies it i.e. unless of course they write in Chinese.

Yet, just to prove that Ray Chow, Amama, and Mr D'Souza had all been to China in reality, let us listen to three observations of Amama about China which will convince one and all that the China sojourn actually did take place. According to Amama's email to...er...his own mama.

a. China is a huge country
b. In China nobody knows where the forks and spoons are hidden
c. No right-minded Chinese person has heard of Kung Pao Chicken or the country of Gyaandostaan

Amama's mama never replied to that email, thus clearing the myth that Amama was a mama's boy. He in fact was just Amama.

Now that we've got the proof out of the way, let's look into the China diary of Ray Chow. The first day was spent sightseeing. This was largely because they couldn't find their hotel. The hotel was supposed to be in a suburb of Beijing. But they discovered soon that 'Mandarin' was a fairly common name for a hotel. Language was a huge issue for our hopeless tourists. And it becomes an even more serious issue for this winter. Chinese dialects and GYAANDOSTAANI had little in common. Ray Chow's grasp of the Chinese language was reprehensible. Mandarin is not pronounced phonetically as Mandarin in Chinese. It has an even more appalling sound in GYAANDOSTAANI.

Then to translate the exchange between locals and our tourists becomes an impossibility. To attempt to print these exchanges could lead to the usage of hundreds of pages, and the subsequent resignation of 4 sub-editors, 2 printers, a printing machine, and 5 interns which although in itself is not such a bad result for this winter, is still a dangerous precedent for books involving different cultures and languages going forward. So, in order not to wreck commerce across the length and breadth of South East Asia, let's cut to the chase. Let's move the story to page 169 (Chinese script), page 243 (Gyaandostaani script) or whatever page number is printed at the bottom of this page. Oops! I know you just checked. Never mind, let's move to a conference room in the Mandarin hotel where the big meeting is engineered between Amama, Mr D'Souza, and Ray Chow with some important Chinese officials. Initially there is a misunderstanding and the meeting is with the catering staff of the hotel, but when two of the Chinese officials drape aprons on Amama and Ray Chow, and a third serves them Peking Duck from Xinhua Province, nowhere next to the erstwhile Peking, the penny drops.

The second meeting is the Real McCoy or more appropriately the real Fa-Hein. Seven Chinese officials dressed in dark suits sat in stoic silence listening to Ray

Chow's presentation. Alongside them was an extremely pretty Chinese girl who was acting as translator. The meeting was like a waltz. A one two and then cha-cha-cha. Ray would say a few words then wail as the pretty translator translated. Then the officials would ask questions, and she would reverse translate to Gyaandostaani. The questions the officials asked were hard-hitting ones, such as:

a. Why can't a man of Chinese descent speak in Chinese?
b. Why was Mr D'Souza asleep?
c. How on earth did Ray Chow have so much hair on his chest?

Ray's presentation itself was the usual humbug of how, under the Ball and Socket Party, China would enjoy the advantage of unrestrained trade, and the right of just refusal to each and all trade and commerce contracts. In lieu of this as a gesture of good faith, if the Chinese could grant 50 million US dollars towards the party's election fund, everybody involved would emerge winners. At this last piece of information, the Chinese officials laughed heartily. Official no. 4 had a hysterical fit while no. 7 may have wet his pants from laughing so hard. No. 7 informed that not only was this a incredulous sum, but more importantly they would be billing the GYAANDOSTAANIS for dinner, though this was a 3 o'clock in the afternoon meeting. At this suggestion, the hysteria started afresh again. Ray Chow and Amama looked disconsolate, defeated even, and then it happened.

Mr D'Souza woke up and started talking in GYAANDOSTAANI. Except no one in the whole world, in any culture or language demographic could actually understand what Mr D' Souza was saying. In actuality, all the old man wanted was a trip to the toilet, but his manner and verbal examination had a cathartic effect, sort of, on the Chinese officials. They loved him. One thought he resembled a chimpanzee who recently tried to mate with a dry fountain in Beijing zoo except the chimp appeared to be a little taller. Another thought he sounded just like the Egyptian ambassador to China who had suffered severe speech impediment after an accident, whilst shaving and brushing his teeth simultaneously. Another felt he resembled his 93-year-old father-in-law who was in an advanced state of Alzheimer's, and thus reminded another official of the said chimpanzee in Beijing Zoo that Mr D'Souza also reminded the previous official off initially. Amama and Ray Chow became redundant. Soon the officials were playing games with Mr D'Souza, getting him to bark like a dog (this was done when he was asked to do his impression of a fish drowning). Then one time he made sounds like a 79-year-old turtle's digestive system. This of course was in response to a request to sing the GYAANDOSTAANI anthem. Whatever it was, they loved him. The meeting continued for hours. The 7 officials and the pretty translator soon invited their friends and family to meet the new star who kept outdoing himself with audio so offensive to the sophisticated ear that it just had to be heard at least once. So deliriously happy were the officials that once they finished taking photographs and videos of this greatest thing since the Great Wall, that they merrily drew up contracts between themselves and the Ball and Socket Party. The effect of these contracts will be felt only at the end of the tale which is either on page 207 (Chinese), 296 (Gyaandostaani), or whenever you decide it should be, dear reader. But more of that later. For now Mr D'Souza had brought two civilizations together simply by his inability to concentrate. In fact, this great success was achieved when all Mr D'Souza was ever trying to do was visit the toilet.

History in fact is replete with miscommunication leading to social success. Alexander thought King Puru was teaching him a classical dancing form. Puru thought Alexander was looking for his mother who had gone missing. And the two men bonded, though no accurate account of their actual conversation has been recorded.

The Ball and Socket Party members meanwhile were not privy to the goings-on in China. This is because back in China, Ray Chow was clinging to an old Chinese proverb that first occurred in Las Vegas: 'What happens in China, stays in China'. They were however privy to the goings-on in the government. Paul showed Colleen a copy of *The Waving Flag*. The front page had a picture of President Jagee in his swim trunks standing arms akimbo on a two-metre diving board. His left foot was bent toward his right knee, and his body was tight and perched to dive. The headlines said, 'The President's new driver. Power to the People.' Paul read out the article aloud:

'President Jagee has done it again. First he gave GYAANDOSTAAN over 40 new card tables to encourage the game of bridge. Then he had all the speed breakers painted black and white. In fact, lets list his achievements first, shall we? He was the first to introduce the pin card no., for your pin card number, thus creating a double lock security for you to fight credit fraud. He was the first to use arrows in the public works department. Now you can tell whether a road is a one way or not, except when it's not. To help with the environment, he came up with the concept of the same T-shirt week where one wears the same T-shirt, Monday to Sunday. His point that if the military could do it, so could we was well documented. He pioneered the discount coupon scheme for vegetarians on every 4th Saturday of the month, thus giving a major fillip to animal awareness. He had substantially helped build relations between GYAANDOSTAAN and several countries. By visiting Japan to play golf on alternate weekends, he'd brought those countries closer. In Canada he owned hotels that gave a 7½ percent discount for Gyaandostaan citizens during summer. In Switzerland he owned two mountains and over a 100 chalets. In France a sea resort. In Australia a chain of shrimp farms. And now this champion of champion is restoring power to people. In an unprecedented move, President Col. Jagee had abolished power cuts, thus making GYAANDOSTAAN the first country in the world to do so. All citizens will, with immediate effect, enjoy unlimited power and electricity, day and night, from this point on. And where are the funds coming from to ensure "Power to the People"? Well, ladies and gentlemen, from our great humanitarian

Col. Jagee himself. He is cancelling his yearly holiday and also selling his malls in Wassaw to ensure that Power to the People becomes his legacy. Col. Jagee's other achievements include:

a. First and only man to fly in a hot air balloon across the length and breadth of Bey. (Readers please note, flying hot air balloons are completely banned in the country of GYAANDOSTAAN.)
b. Underwater holding breath champion. 73½ seconds; a GYAANDOSTAANI record.
c. GYAANDOSTAANI record of standing on only his left foot for 2 hours 37 minutes, without taking any support. (The support was of course removed with that modern miracle—photoshop.)
d. Only GYAANDOSTAANI to fight and maim a man eating tiger in Bangladesh when on a youth tour (even though the video evidence of this fight has been lost, there is absolutely no need to doubt him). Got his flying license at 14. His matriculation at 13. Wrote his first book at 10 and shaved for the first time at 7½ years of age. Clearly the first citizen of GYAANDOSTAAN. Now, with the "Power to the People", he's joining the ranks of Benjamin Disraeli, Thomas Jefferson, Ben Franklin, Mikhail Gorbachev, and Nelson

Mandela himself as a great statesman in their very likeness.'

Colleen reacted appropriately, making sounds like she was gagging and needed to throw up. There was nothing more to do. A meeting, an emergency meeting, was called between the SWIM brothers, Shampoo, and the Ball and Socket Party.

The SWIM brothers couldn't catch a break since the tone of voice Paul and Colleen used scared them to their white socks. They tried to merge with the grey sofa, but to no avail. The next time they checked, they were still there with Paul, Colleen, Shabbir Hossein, and Bella Terrace. Since all 4 were asking them questions at the same time, the SWIM brothers started experiencing their hourly anxiety attack. You could spot a SWIM brother anxiety attack a mile away.

Their heads would slowly slip inside their starched white collars simultaneously. By rendering themselves headless, they imagined they wouldn't have to answer any questions. In much the way an ostrich buries his head in the sand to fool the lioness into thinking the rest of him is not an ostrich. A ploy that has worked once every twelve thousand times. But Paul Huskee was on the attack.

Paul: 'There is no way the "Power to the People" concept could've come from that nincompoop. You have to have suggested it.'

Colleen: 'And for God's sake get you heads out of your collars and pretend you are real men.'

To be fair, when Paul was speaking, there was some signage, some movement, to suggest heads would pop back out to their original positions, but the moment Colleen's ordering started, the head stripped back with a boomerang effect to way below collar level and relative safety ensconced in the middle of the shirt. So it was up to Bella Terrace—the voice of reason. She was the most experienced and decided to go for tact and a more mature approach.

Bella Terrace: 'I will count to 5. Just to 5. By 5 if your heads aren't out of your shirts, they will be NEVER coming out. Comprende hombres?' Bella Terrace's love affair with the Spaghetti Western needs a mention here.

The last two words made little sense as the SWIM name was not really used in any Latin language. Latin or not, the SWIM brothers finally did react to this new threat. This they did by sinking even lower, miraculously (though no substantive proof is available), into possibly their trouser territory.

At this, Bella Terrace and Colleen started to take matters into their own hands. Their hands entered the collars of the SWIM brothers in a 'flushing out' operation that could end only one way, with the ostriches suffering some form of cardiac arrest. Just as the SWIM brothers were about to meet a horrible end, Shampoo burst through the door. Hurriedly, he explained that all was well, and how the President was going to change astronomical rates for power post elections, so all they really had to do was make a public promise that his offer would hold good in the new term, failing which he would be forced to abdicate the throne.

As calmness returned to the Ball and Socket Party, the SWIM brothers simultaneously thanked everyone from deep inside their white shirts and made quick their exit. Call it...er....a headstart, but they needed to put some distance between themselves and all political parties for the time. Back at the Ball and Socket headquarters, Paul started formulating his plan.

Paul: 'We've got a three-pronged platform with which we'll attack him. One—failed promises. Two—corruption and nepotism using public machinery for personal gain. Three—lunacy; he wears no clothes, makes ridiculous gestures, has no respect for the law and is, if subjected to the appropriate tests, certifiably insane.'

12

Ray Chow was really happy with himself. China had been a super success. He came back with various trade contacts, the biggest being that the GYAANDOSTAAN based Ball and Socket Party would now be the sole providers of woollen socks to every single province, village, and city in China. Woollen socks were very popular in China, and were always in short supply. Getting this monopoly could make the economy of a small country like GYAANDOSTAAN. The math was mind boggling—with 1.3 billion people in China, and with most having two feet, 2.6 million socks had to be made and sold on a yearly basis. GYAANDOSTAAN had a substance, a sap from their Ligor trees which, when hardened and treated chemically, came to resemble wool. The whole process was cheaper than using sheep. And unlike sheep who were available everywhere, Ligor was native only to

GYAANDOSTAAN. They would thus gain support of the second most powerful lobby in the world, after the defence lobby—the animal rights' lobby.

The *Glasnost Times* carried a full front page story replete with photos of Ray Chow's successful conquest of China. The pictures included Ray Chow leaning on the Great Wall, sailing on the Yang Tse river, attending a Chinese opera in Shanghai, and in China Valley (the last one being a popular restaurant in Bey, but nobody seemed to notice).

The *Glasnost Times* spoke of how, with the thousands of acres of Ligor trees that the Huskee family owned, there was going to be a woollen revolution, and GYAANDOSTAAN would do business of 5.2 billion dollars a year from the woollen sock trade, at the very least. More than tripling the entire business model of the present government under Col. Jagee.

Also mentioned in the article was how Mr D'Souza brought honour to GYAANDOSTAAN, having earned China's highest possible award, 'The Ment of China', for no particular reason. He also became the brand ambassador for a variety of Chinese products, including an acupuncture company, a phone answering service, and for Chinese tourism. In fact, so successful and popular had Mr D'Souza become that Ray Chow had to commit the ultimate sacrifice and leave him behind in Beijing to carry out his various commitments and just to ensure he didn't get lost, Amama was also detained to chaperon China's favourite foreign son.

Amama then got into the act, and started marketing their new cash cow. An audio tape entitled 'Mr D'Souza Says' became a game changer. In this tape, Mr D'Souza recorded famous Gyaandostaani-to-Chinese phrases. The tape sold out in 16 minutes flat. And this in a country where no one owned tape recorders anymore. Amama then charged exorbitantly for public appearances and Mr D'Souza was well on his way to becoming a prominent industry on his own. Although he did think it a trifle peculiar that tourists in China were themselves subject to be photo grouped continuously and encouraged to talk on P.A. systems to large crows of citizens.

Col. Jagee stormed: 'AMERICA. They've got China. We'll get America.'

Shampoo immediately pointed out the real problem with this plan. Col. Jagee was banned from entering America for 20 years, 9 of which were still left.

Col. Jagee: 'India. Let's get India.'

Shampoo: 'India? Nobody does business with India. Nobody knows who's in-charge.'

Col. Jagee: 'Japan?'

Shampoo: 'You're on their "No Fly" list.'

Col. Jagee: 'South Korea?'

Shampoo: 'They won't even pick up our phones.'

Col. Jagee: 'Okay Canada, then we've already had their top dog over, so let's get Canada to play ball.

Col. Jagee had just entered his Julius Caesar phase. Somebody had taken him to a production of Julius Caesar in Europe and Col. Jagee was in love almost immediately. Now, dressed in a brown Toga, he was toying with the idea of wearing a laurel wreath. Then better sense prevailed and he removed the Toga and wore just the laurel wreath.

Col. Jagee: 'Think of what trade we can set up with Canada that'll net us billions in dollars? What are they in need of?'

Shampoo: 'People.'

Col. Jagee: 'Okay, let's give them people. How much can we charge per person? Roughly?'

Shampoo: 'You mean sell Gyaandostaani citizens to Canada?'

Col. Jagee: 'Yes, at least a thousand dollars a man?'

Shampoo: 'You mean like slaves?'

Col. Jagee: 'Yes, slaves exactly. So thousand for men and fifteen hundred for women? What's a million multiplied by thousand?'

Shampoo: 'Sir I don't think we can just sell people. In today's day and age, it's a lot more complicated than that.'

Col. Jagee: 'Don't be negative. Canada wasn't built in a day.'

As they talked, Shampoo slowly convinced the great leader to put on his Toga. More advisors were called in and Col. Jagee outlined his master plan. As he put it, people were more expensive than socks. And more of a nuisance. If over a three-year plan three million Gyaandostaanis could be sold off to Canada, they'd be rolling in it. But one million was a lot in a country of roughly forty million. Shampoo tried to explain that while he was dressing as Julius Caesar, and morphing occasionally into Mussolini. The Sandwich Party, as timble as it was, wasn't quite the Third Reich. However, Col. Jagee couldn't be talked out of it. He saw only advantages to the plan such as all members of the party could make lists of people they wanted to have disappear to Canada. In fact he got so excited by this last thought that he himself immediately started scribbling down his own list.

Finally, with great difficulty, Shampoo convinced Jagee that such a plan would only be feasible with the consent of Canada.

Shampoo: 'Sir, first and foremost you'll have to visit Canada before we take this any further.'

Col. Jagee: 'Okay, great, not a problem. Let's take the bull by the horns. Er...just one...er...thing...'

Shampoo: 'Yes, Sir?'

Col. Jagee: 'Am I banned in Canada?'

13

14th of May midnight was a very important date in the GYAANDOSTAANI calendar. It was on this day that the Macedonian army beat a retreat from the country that today is called GYAANDOSTAAN. Okay, this is historically not that accurate. Nobody knows when or why the Macedonians left. From all accounts the locals begged them not to. After all, it was the Macedonians who went about constructing things like medical shelters, places of study, bridges, roads, wine shops, and amphitheatres. In fact, they were so loved that every local family adopted a Macedonian soldier. It is said the soldier's every whim was catered to. If one took a bath, he wouldn't have to use his own hands, to give just one example.

Macedonian historian Rahaesphan said, 'Their beards were too tightly strung.' This is an old Macedonian saying which means the soldiers were feeling suffocated.

Some tried to drown themselves, while others started disguising themselves as village womenfolk. This does explain why in parts of Gyaandostaan some women still have strong Macedonian features. Many said they had to see a man about a dog after which they would leave the house, never to return, and march straight back to Macedonia. Whatever the true nature of their exit, GYAANDOSTAANI politicians, using the best tool available to a politician—fiction—created a National Independence Day.

The month of May was chosen after much careful deliberation. The sole basis of this deliberation was Rahaesphan's monumental treatise of the country titled *1,879 Parallels Between Hell And GYAANDOSTAAN*, a statistic that was strongly questioned by the Scottish Historian William McStatt in his fine historical masterpiece, *Rahaesphan Was Wrong: There are 2276 Parallels Between Hell and GYAANDOSTAAN* although his sequel *I Was Wrong: There Are 3964 Parallels Between Hell and GYAANDOSTAAN* was the book that brought GYAANDOSTAAN into the light of the modern world.

Back to Rahaesphan's epic work, the month of May was chosen as this word 'May' was the word mentioned most (22,596) times in the book *1,879 Parallels*

Between Hell And GYAANDOSTAAN, though not on one of the occasions was it ever used as a noun.

Clearly, the facts are hoary. But hoary and GYAANDOSTAAN were two peas in the pod. But why the history lesson? Well, dear reader, because finally, and this time one is forced to swear on all that is sacred, the story starts from here. This date, 14th May, 20 and something, is when our tale basically unfolds. Forget what you've read before. I most definitely have. And I've written some of it. It all begins on the 14th of May.

I'm sure you've guessed it already. Just in case you haven't, let me explain further. The 14th of May was also Parliamentary Games Day in GYAANDOSTAAN. That's right—a day when the entire parliament is cajoled into taking part in an athletics programme at the famous Col. Jagee Park overlooking the beautiful Bey Valley where the Parliamentary Games were enacted. Year after year.

In true athletic tradition, Col. Jagee would 'fix' all the events, thus ensuring his favourites would win all the laurels. Thus it was a matter of great prestige to win in an event at the Parliamentary Games. For the last seven years, Col. Jagee himself won the 100-metres race and bear in mind that in three of the seven years he hadn't even turned up for the competition. The events of course were a mixture of old, traditional, and new.

The old were the sprints. The traditional included the coconut water race where you drank up the coconut water using a straw in your nostril. The new included events like who can last longer in a cage with a boa constrictor. Again, in the last case, Col. Jagee himself was a worthy return winner every single year. In fact at this particular event, his confidence was so high that this year he insisted on having a boa constrictor in his cage that was alive!

Though after his aides showed him what a boa constrictor could do to a large watermelon (possibly the closest living thing to Col. Jagee at that time), he was more than happy to turn back to plan 'A'.

This May 14th, the Parliamentary Games were going to have a different hue. The Ball and Socket Party were on the rise and soon Col. Jagee would be wishing he was the watermelon instead. It was all down to the obstacle relay. The Ball and Socket Party, which, under the unbalanced Machado, would lose and lose badly every single time to the Sandwich Party, was gung-ho and on a mission. Firstly, the obstacle relay squad had a new look about them. Shabbir Hoosein,

Ray Chow, the just-returned-from-China Amama, and Paul Huskee looked relatively fitter and pretty ship-shape compared to the Sandwich Squad comprising of Col. Jagee, his trusted untrusty aide Shampoo, and the SWIM brothers. The latter much to their chagrin.

The SWIM brothers were mortified of open places, and weren't used to the sun, whose bright appearance at 9 o'clock in the morning added to their fear and anxiety. How they begged Col. Jagee to let them off the hook, but unfortunately, gripped by anxiety and paralyzed by fear at the advancing President of GYAANDOSTAAN, no actual formal words were able to leave their mouths. Instead, long-held same-sounding syllables took their place. And it's difficult to make a strong point to a President of a country with a lengthy ooooooo, much less a well held, 'eouuuuuu'. Now before we enjoy the race, let's understand the events in the event, so to speak.

Obstacle relay took its name from old GYAANDOSTAANI rituals which included, but were not restricted to, getting up, washing hands, and brushing teeth. Legend has it (apparently legend always has it) that the Macedonians who occupied ancient GYAANDOSTAAN were the first civilized race (uncivilized races were brushing their teeth as well as other body parts from time immemorial) to actually clean their teeth.

They were forced to do that because of the sediment that stuck to them after they bathed in the KWONGEK river. This was done using the world's first ever toothbrush, a GYAANDOSTAANI local's fingers. Sometimes with the GYAANDOSTAANI local's permission.

In the present obstacle relay, 4 participants per team were used. The first leg consisted of covering a contestant in soot and then pushing him into a khaki sack. The sack was spun around 3 times, and then the disoriented occupants had to bounce toward the 100 metre line. Many of them obviously would go in the wrong direction. Some to never be seen again. However, if you made it to the second leg, i.e. the 100-metre mark, the next contestant would have to remove the man from the sack, brush off all his soot, including that found on his teeth, after which both would have to climb into the sack together and hobble off to the 200 metre mark. Here, they were greeted by their third partner, who would place the sack and its occupants in a Tuk Tuk (like the ones found on the streets of Bangkok in the days of old when there was no emergency declaration). He would then hand pull the Tuk Tuk to the 300-metre mark line where he too would get into the sack. This is where the final team member came in. Using only his feet, he would have to kick the sack with the three occupants all the way to the finish line. It was not so much a matter of getting to the finish line as much as it was about actually finishing the race. To ensure the race was just and fair, Col. Jagee's people ensured that the opponents got smaller sacks.

This year the packed stadium were in for a shock as they would be privy to an actual competition race.

The Ball and Socket gang were in the third lane. In the 4th premiere lane was Col. Jagee and his team. When the race was about to commence, Col. Jagee's team started to hand out the sacks. Col. Jagee beamed at his overconfident team, like the look a tiger gives when killing a deer with a case of multiple paralysis. However, Col. Jagee was in for a rude shock when Paul Huskee pulled out his own custom-made sacks. An argument ensued. The rule book was pulled out. Paul Huskee explained that it was clearly stated in the rules that whoever got the higher sponsorship had the right to provide the apparatus for the competition. What Col. Jagee didn't know was that the company 'GYAANDOSTAAN'S VELCRO' was an extension of the *Forbes* Top 10 MNC based in China—the Hing Hing Corporation—and that the Ball and Socket were their long arm in India. They were the sponsors for the GYAANDOSTAANI Parliamentary Games. The deal had been inked and signed by Col. Jagee himself.

Col. Jagee recalled the day he did and cursed himself for not reading the fine print. The money that had been returned to him (unsubstantiated rumours say 65 hundred thousand Ragoos) caused him to believe the deal was above board, honest, and most importantly, completely favourable to him. He cursed himself for wearing underpants that day. He had long before established a correlation between clothes and brain activity. The less clothes, the better the brain activity. He made a mental note to have underwear banned nationally somewhere down the line. In the meantime, Amama was handing out the new sacks which were folded into the size of a small handkerchief. This was held tightly in place by a series of knots which would take an average engineering graduate roughly 45 minutes to unravel. As the other teams started experimenting with their sacks, Col. Jagee was getting more and more agitated. Shampoo wasn't making much headway. So Col. Jagee asked the SWIM brothers to do the needful. However, the SWIM brothers had just declared a state of emergency. They had been asked to separate and occupy different positions, one brother at the starting point of the race, and the second a good 100 meters away. As mentioned four times before, and once in this book, the SWIM brothers never separated, not to use the toilet, not to eat a meal, not even to surf highly illegal material on the net.

In fact, they were so close to actually overcoming fear and finally throwing a tantrum. Then fear won, and one of the SWIM brothers fainted, the one on the right. That is the one on the right of the one on the left. This did nothing for Col. Jagee's mood. And then for Col. Jagee, almost in slow motion, the whistle blew.

And the race had started. As Shabbir Hoosein reached the 100-metre mark, none of the others had even managed to open their sacks (when translated back into GYAANDOSTAANI, there is no question of a pun). Highly muffed, Col. Jagee ordered for a pair of scissors. Even as they cut open the sack, Amama had reached the 200-metre mark along with Shabbir Hoosein.

The Sandwich Party's gentler elements placed a SWIM brother's still body on the hundred mark line. Meanwhile the one on the right of the one previously on the left, covered with soot, entered the sack. After being spun around, he was off, never to be seen again. Okay, that's an exaggeration. He was found the following Tuesday. In the meanwhile, to the roar of a packed stadium, Paul Huskee, Ray Chow, Shabbir Hoosein, and Amama pushed past the finish line. Only Amama complained. That is because he was right at the top of the sack, the joint where Paul Huskee's boot made unfailing and repetitive contact. The Ball and Socket Party did a lap of honour, with only Shabbir Hoosein being left in the sack as his arms had been badly entangled in the knots. But even he, rolling around on his torso in a Khakhi shelter, was enjoying the obvious support and goodwill of the crowd. In the meantime Col. Jagee was being held back by Shampoo and others who were vainly pointing out that choking this SWIM brother for the other SWIM brother's disappearance was perhaps a crime. Not that it mattered to the one on the left of the one of the right. He was out for the count. The big worry for Col. Jagee was, so it appeared, his Sandwich Party.

The *Glasnost Times* was very specific in its headlines. 'No meat in Sandwich Party'. 'Party's performance left between the breads'. The editor Andrei used a lot of mixed metaphors about Col. Jagee's impending demise in his editorial. 'The Bull was caught well and truly with

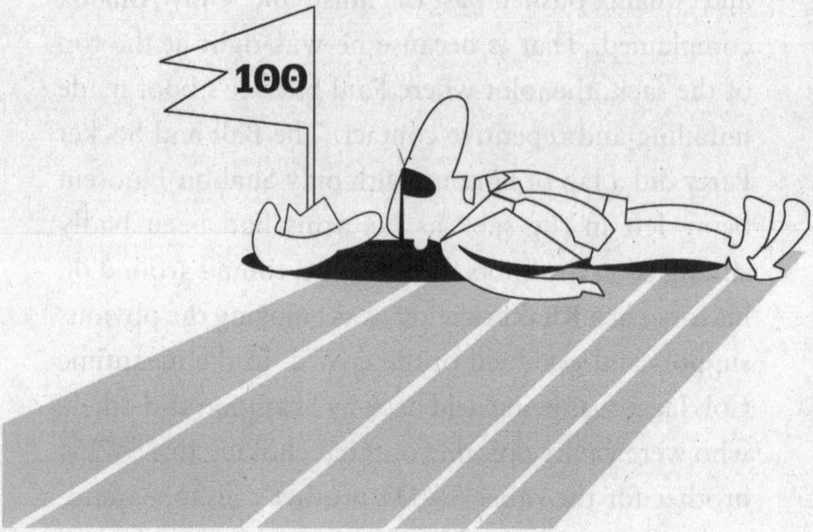

The Sandwich Party's gentler elements placed a Swim brother's still body on the hundred mark line.

his pants down' being amongst the nicer references.

GYAANDOSTAAN was by no means a great sporting nation. They had only twice before qualified for the Olympic games. And their performance was so poor that it was said they even failed the march past.

Let's move now to Col. Jagee's quarters where he was perusing the two newspapers. The *Waving Flag* didn't even mention the Parliamentary Games, which was strange as they were one of the sponsors. Col. Jagee was so angry and seething that he had donned a bathrobe. Someone had told him it belonged to Chengiz Khan's grandson, Hugulu. How a GYAANDOSTAANI citizen came to inherit a 800-year-old piece of clothing was not very clear. Also how a Mongol Prince got his hands on a terry cotton bathrobe 800 years ago was even murkier. As any Mongol historian would tell you, Hugulu hated baths. And besides, you didn't put the fear of God in all of Central Asia and South East Europe by prancing around in a purple bath robe, not in those days at least. Not unless this was a precursor to a mating ritual.

The Col. bit his lip and spat at Gomango Bosh. Gomango looked at Shampoo for support, but Shampoo was busy sending a picture of Hugulu

Jagee to Paul Huskee on his phone. In order to earn compassion, Gomango Bosh started coughing. Really coughing, with the odd sneeze and shiver thrown in to compound the effect. But Hugulu Jagee was in no mood to take prisoners.

Col. Jagee: 'The Parliamentary Games are our greatest cultural extravaganza. After fixing them for 40 years, how did we mess it up? Who is responsible?'

Gomango Bosh knew the obvious answer was to show Hugulu a picture of himself but better sense prevailed. And remember our Hugulu wasn't as balanced as the original Hulugu.

Gomango Bosh: 'President Sir, why are you looking behind?'

To this Col. Jagee cast a sheepish cursory glance behind himself.

Gomango Bosh: 'It's not my place as public prosecutor to advise you, but I'm told by others that since the momentum is with Ball and Socket, maybe it's best to reconcile with them. Put out the olive branch, so to speak.'

To this Col. Jagee sprang out of his bathrobe and was absolutely beside himself. Meanwhile Shampoo quickly clicked a new picture of the wannabe Mongol overlord, and quickly doused the flames.

Shampoo: 'I've got some good news, Col. Jagee, and it's just outside your office.'

This seemed to have the desired effect on Col. Jagee. He wore the bathrobe again and sank back into his chair.

Col. Jagee: 'What is it? Have the SWIM brothers been located and flogged?'

Shampoo: 'Better, much better. See for yourself.'

With this Shampoo opened the door and a young, extremely effete man entered. He had on a multi-coloured pair of jeans and a leopard print t-shirt, but it was the straw hat which gave Mohan Huskee that really outlandish look.

Shampoo: 'Col. Jagee, Gomango Bosh, please meet Mohan Huskee, the youngest of all the Huskees, who has left the Ball and Socket Party and has defected to the Sandwich Party.'

Mohan Huskee was effete and feminine. He made Shampoo look like Chengiz Khan himself. Col. Jagee's mood changed immediately. If there were cracks in the Huskee family, this would only be good news for him.

Col. Jagee: 'Welcome Mohan (In GYAANDOSTAANI the A in Mohan was silent so the sound was more Mohn. In fact, in the Gyaandostaan alphabet, lots of letters were silent. This was a cause of great confusion, especially if your name was made up of all such silent alphabets.), lovely to have you. How is your brother, father, mother, and grandfather?'

Mohan Huskee courtisied and began his sad tale. He spoke of how he had always been sidelined in the Huskee household. When he wanted to pursue dancing, he was denied. His collection of poetry titled *Love on a Stationary Cycle* had also been denied publishing. His paintings, which were a tribute to the nude form of males in their seventies, were never encouraged. It all reached a head when he asked Paul to consider him for Deputy President if the Ball and Socket Party came to power. He spoke of how enraged he was when Paul's answer was to laugh loudly for 15 minutes consecutively and then hold his head in a bucket of water. He shared how he didn't mind being suffocated and humiliated by his brother. But when Amama and Ray Chow removed his trousers and tattooed Deputy President on his posterior, he felt quite ashamed. But even this was bearable. It's just when Bella Terrace and Shabbir Hoosein tied him to a car and dragged him around their parking lot that something in him snapped, and though he thought it was his spinal cord, it couldn't have been, because that snapped a long time ago. Years of humiliation had finally gotten to him and so here he was, with vital information for Col. Jagee. Information that would cause Col. Jagee great joy. In return, all he wanted was a Deputy Presidentship or a cabinet portfolio. And regarding the latter, he didn't want 'Defence' as he didn't like guns. He also didn't want 'Home' as he liked to step out a little and he didn't want 'Parliamentary Affairs' as he didn't know what it meant.

Col. Jagee stopped laughing for a second and said, 'Oh, you're being serious?'

Mohan Huskee: 'Do you know my parents made me swap my birthday with Paul? I'm July born, and his is Feb 29th. Since his is on a leap year, they celebrate his on 11th July and mine once every four years only.'

Col. Jagcc (by now smiling and beaming): 'It's a travesty, a blot against all the collective laws of natural justice. But, without sounding disrespectful, what information could you possibly give me that will bring Paul Huskee to his knees, except maybe spondylitis?'

Mohan Huskee: 'What I give you will assure you victory at the next elections. That's what information I got.'

Nobody was laughing now. Hugulu Jagee fastened his bathrobe belt in such a way it covered his navel, but left the above and below relatively free. But Col.

Jagee was, for the first time in a long time, feeling a little triumphant. Hope had come from unexpected quarters. Mohan may have been a non-entity. In fact he was so under the radar that for 4 years in a row in his childhood, his family forgot to pay his school fees. The colonel made a decision. He opened his bathrobe belt.

Col. Jagee: 'If what you say helps us to win, the Deputy Presidency is yours. What do you think, Governor?'

Gomango Bosh: 'Well, first I want to know how a grown man can actually have a 24-inch waist.'

It was true. Mohan Huskee was the thinnest person in all of GYAANDOSTAAN, if you don't count the people depicted in paintings and stick figures found in the ancient caves of South West GYAANDOSTAAN.

Mohan Huskee: 'What I'm about to tell you must stay in this room.' He said this with the authority and confidence of a one-legged acrobat about to walk a tight rope blindfolded and 3,000 feet from the earth.

Col. Jagee, Gomango Bosh, and Shampoo all nodded in approval and collectively moved closer. Why this is done in human behaviour is unclear. But suffice to say that when one human is about to tell an earth-shattering story like revealing his birth mother's true gender, the group for some reason closes in on him.

Animals like hyenas do the same thing. Though it must be said amongst hyenas if gossip is not appreciated, then the rest of the hyenas urinate on the one chanting the gossip gospel, which in hyena society is not necessarily a sign of disapproval, unless it happens twice on the same day.

Mohan Huskee: 'As you've guessed after the Parliamentary Games, the Ball and Socket Party has made a killing on their deal with China. The figure is astonishing, and they are going to use their money to aggressively market their campaign and wipe-out not just the Sandwich Party but sandwiches from the face of the earth. They've collected the entire signing amount which comes to 30 million US dollars. However, they've invested the money in The People's Democratic Bank of Liberal North Korea where Kim Jong Sul the third has promised 33 percent interest rate per year on any sum of money over 10 million dollars invested in this bank. In fact, the money of all the major governments are now parked in North Korea. The idea is to pull out the money at the time you announce elections only, then using that money power to devour the Sandwich Party once and for all.'

Col. Jagee didn't like this. Why did Mohan Huskee

have to be so graphic? He swallowed the air and asked Mohan Huskee to continue.

Mohan Huskee: 'Well Sir, you have a window of opportunity. You see from tomorrow North Korea is closed for renovation.'

Col. Jagee: 'Closed for renovation?'

Mohan Huskee: 'Yes, every year on Kim Jong Sul the third's (he killed the first?) birthday, North Korea is shut for five days in a period known as "renovation". Renovation signifies some act or event that goes on per day which is supposed to improve and better society in North Korea. On day 1 he purges the country of evil relatives. This includes relatives that have committed crimes such as walking in front of him for a second or so, or wearing the same coloured hat as him, or for renting the same movie a second time in a row. The method of execution varies. Bad relatives are shot. Very bad are fed to starving animals. The worst ones are fed to starving relatives. All the executions are watched live on TV and all have great advertising and great amount of sponsorship. On day 2, Kim Jong Sul the third executes all his corrupt officials. This is done in an intelligent, scientific, and precise manner. By choosing names randomly out of yellow pages, if they turn out to be office bearers, Kim Jong Sul the third gives himself a star; if not, he executes them anyway for wasting his time.

'On day 3, it's time for celebrations. This is his actual birthday. Kim Jong Sul the third organizes grand buffets across the length and breadth of the country. To make sure citizens can eat in peace, all beggars and foreigners are rounded up and shot. To give them a fair trial, all foreigners are asked if they are foreigners or beggars. Then in keeping with North Korean tradition, they are shot regardless of their answers.

'Day 4 is a recovery day. All citizens are supposed to stay indoors at home and recover from the birthday celebrations. If you are found loitering, you are given two choices. You are questioned and then shot, or just shot.

'On day 5...'

At this Col. Jagee had heard enough. He burst through his bathrobe, stood up, and scowled. 'What has all this got to do with me? I have very little interest in Kim Jong Sul the third.'

Mohan Huskee: 'Well Sir, if you announce spot elections, sort of flash elections, conduct and finish the proceedings in the next 5 days, then the Ball and

Socket will not be able to avail of any funds. Basically, they are penniless this particular week.'

Col. Jagee: 'Well, Gomango? Shampoo?'

Gomango Bosh: 'I see, interesting (here he had a long thoughtful pause). And what exactly on day 5?'

Col. Jagee: 'Forget day 5. Can we conduct an election in say the next 48 hours?'

Gomango Bosh: 'It's never been done before?'

Shampoo: 'I think it's a ridiculous idea. How do we know this is the truth?'

Gomango Bosh: 'We can check with Pying Pyong. Although it would help to know about day 5...'

Col. Jagee: 'I don't want to hear about day 5. This is a great opportunity, gentleman. I need to know if we can logistically do this in one slam, bang, dunk. Shampoo, get the boys inside...no wait...let's put it to vote, Gomango?

Gomango Bosh: 'Let's not do it. Besides, we haven't yet heard from day 5.'

Col. Jagee: 'I never want to hear that number again. Shampoo?'

Shampoo: 'I'm going with Gomango. Let's avoid this. It's too rushed.'

Col. Jagee: 'Okay, I'm for it. So it's pretty clear then. We'll announce the elections immediately. Thanks for coming, Mohan and Shampoo. Find Mohan a bathrobe in his size. He's one of us now. Thank you Mohan.'

Surprisingly for once, Mohan Huskee didn't want to be hugged by a naked man and stood his ground.

14

The *Waving Flag* put out a full-page advertisement.

Elections to be held on Wednesday, in all 43 provinces of GYAANDOSTAAN.

'Dear citizens, my friends, brothers, and sisters. Due to impending weather conditions and technical reasons, I'm forced to hold our general elections within the next 48 hours. The actual time for casting the ballot will be 11:09 am to 3:27 pm on Wednesday this week. Although this puts the Sandwich Party at a great disadvantage as we've had no time to prepare, let me warn all players that the candidates and parties must provide a complete and detailed list of those canvassing by 4 pm tomorrow at the New Custom House "C" wing, which is where the Election Commission is located. Any complaints or queries must be addressed to Mr Gomango Bosh, Mr Shampoo, and Mr Mohan

Huskee, who are the democratically elected, neutral, election office bearers.

'Mr Bosh as you know is our public prosecutor, Mr Shampoo is now my chief political aide, and Mr Mohan Huskee I'm told is a male.

'To avoid any unlawful occurrences and confrontations, here are a list of guidelines all participants in this major, mega extravaganza must adhere to.

1. *All candidates must appear in public in long pants at all times.*
2. *Those who are left-handed must declare so in their application letter.*
3. *No candidates or their party members or their supporters thereof should be found loitering around the election centres. Obviously, this rule does not apply to members and supporters of the ruling partly due to technical reasons such as having to simultaneously conduct the elections as well as deal with prevailing weather conditions at the time.*
4. *No party supporter or member should stop citizens from entering poll booths. Obviously, the ruling party members are exempt from this rule due to technical reasons such as having to*

personally provide security at the booths as well as deal with prevailing weather conditions at the time.

5. *Citizens are told to observe basic decorum. They are not to spit, swear, and relieve themselves in the polling booth. They must, if possible, also avoid spitting, swearing, and relieving themselves on opposition candidates. This obviously doesn't hold good for the ruling party who due to technical reasons such as long hours are left with no chance but to spit, swear, and relieve themselves on other people.*
6. *If weather conditions are unbearable, the last election results will be held as valid. To make this a free and fair election, the weather comptroller is Mr Shampoo and that final decision will be made by him.*
7. *Obese people, slow learners, people with acne, and little people may be disbarred from voting according to the discretion of the polling booth officer.'*

The rest of the paper had large pictures of Col. Jagee and some key party members. For some strange reason, Col. Jagee was in a strange set of progressive undress. Col. Jagee at the National Day parade in full regalia;

Col. Jagee with his horses; Col. Jagee at the beach; Col. Jagee in the bubble bath, minus the bubbles; Col. Jagee in bed.

To balance it out, to be completely fair, Paul Huskee was also given some footage. A picture of a completely 'wasted' Paul Huskee lying on his back on the floor, with Colleen Connor's foot on his chest, appeared under the caption of other 'aspiring' candidates.

Col. Jagee was readying for battle. Unbeknownst to him, the battle had long since begun.

GYAANDOSTAAN went berserk. For the next three days, it became like a state undergoing a 'good' emergency. Schools, colleges, and banks, in fact all commercial institutions, remained closed. There was a flurry of activities on the street, as candidates jousted with each other for prominent banners. In GYAANDOSTAAN, it was not uncommon for one banner to cover another one as candidates tried to outdo one another. In the spirit of free and fair, not to mention an extremely dignified elective process, different techniques were evolving. One such was the 'Black Ink Gang'. They were a group of affluent investment bankers who offered their services during campaigning, not as bankers but as gangs of thugs who would blacken with ink the banner of a candidate for a certain fee. They often worked at cross-purposes, as bankers often do, and would take on as rivals both opposition candidates simultaneously, thus in one swoop proving the ultimate aim of politics—to make money regardless of government political situation, clime, or time.

Then there was the 'Mixed Double Coop'. This was a group of ladies who would, again for a considerable fee, slap charges of illicit affairs with sitting MPs as well as new challengers. The fee depended wholly on the aesthetic situation of the candidate. The uglier the candidate, the higher the fee. The young Mr Machado was an early casualty. Early on in his political career, he was weighed down with seven such affairs. So distraught was he by this aerial bombardment that he confessed to five. It was the beginning of the end, resulting ultimately in his vassal state and mental disintegration.

But the most important log in the elective wheel was the fixer Joey Dis who along with his brother Joet Dat and Joey Joey played the role of political brokers.

Joey Dis and his brothers ran the most important business in parliament. They were in charge of the MP's lockers. 300 lockers of 300 members of Parliament were all maintained by Joey Dis and family. That meant, whatever secrets that a particular MP had in his locker was known to Joey Dis. And the secrets were quite varied to be fair. They ranged from a 'How to make a risotto in 4 minutes' recipe to pictures of Col. Jagee watering his plants in the buff. From a sample of pigeon droppings to pictures of an MP before he became a female. The bottom line was Joey Dis and Joey Dat, not to forget Joey Joey, were in a splendid position to buy, sell, and haggle the process of all members of parliament.

In years gone by, this was all one-way traffic, i.e how much to pay an MP to defect to the Sandwich Party? The community charged the most, of course. There were all kinds of stuff available on the menu as the Joeys offered a large à la carte as well as buffet options. You could

a. Get a minister for your birthday party.
b. Stay in a ministerial bungalow for a weekend getaway with your family.
c. Actually take the minister's place for a session in parliament.

d. Have the minister grace your corporate function, where obviously the price would be less if he is allowed to speak.
e. Spend the day swimming with a minister in a seaside resort, as long as in doing so the marine life of the area is not endangered.
f. Be a part of a minister's family function.
g. Get to wake up a member of parliament from his bed. The most expensive, and strangely most popular included, comb a minister's hair, massage a member of parliament and the big one, take the measurements by tape of your favourite member of parliament.

On Tuesday, the day before the actual elections, Joey Dis was inundated by phone calls. He took only the most important one, his hairdresser's. Joey Dis didn't believe in business on the phone. His method was straightforward—you come to him, name your price, and the minister. Then Joey Dat and Joey Joey check with the said minister; they then tell Joey Dis if it's a show, or no go.

But this time, Joey Dis had broken all rules. Bella Terrace, his classmate from GYAANDOSTAAN University, and the love of his life, unbeknownst to Mrs Dis, had camped at his headquarters for the period. The period of the election that is (wise guy). So enamoured with Bella Terrace was Joey Dis that he let lesser sense prevail and soon Bella was in charge of all negotiations. She arranged for 50 Sandwich Party candidates to disappear from the contest. They gladly accepted their paid vacations to different ends of earth. Next up, 35 Sandwich Party sureties were convinced to switch parties. This was done in two steps. First by telling them to. Second by paying them huge sums of money. But that was not the coup de grâce. This was. Every time a Sandwich Party member came to meet Joey Dis, he was ushered into the waiting room as Joey Dis was too busy. At one point Bella Terrace was told that as many as 57 Sandwich MPs were waiting to meet Joey Dis. Many had been waiting for over 10 hours. Bella Terrace felt bad and decided enough was enough. They already had the numbers, there was no need to be insensitive. The Sandwich guys were waiting for hours. So finally, she offered them tea. Now you might, dear reader, raise a very important point which I hadn't noticed. In which case you may raise another even more important point which again may have escaped my attention. So finally you may scream that Joey's love for Bella could only take them so far. Ultimately he was and is a businessmen and would want hard currency for his one-sided favouritism. Then you would make your second point (and I applaud you on this one because it means you've been paying attention as clearly as I haven't been, and thank God one of us is for the sake of this book), which would be that if the Ball and Socket Party's money is tied up in the North Korea's leader's birthday celebrations, then where is the money coming from to buy all these members of Parliament love or no love? Members of parliament don't grow on trees, you know. To answer your very important points, we need to relocate ourselves to the home of the great leader (great leader according to a survey conducted of himself by himself)—Col. Jagee, President of GYAANDOSTAAN.

15

Midnight, Tuesday, February 20 and something, to be precise. President Jagee, the only Colonel in GYAANDOSTAAN military who had never seen a single active day of service, was at his wits' end. Wearing his Saddam Hussein fatigues, complete with a beret, he was tapping his desk with his feet. But that wasn't the peculiar part. The peculiar part was he was standing on it.

Col. Jagee: 'Are you telling me Shampoo that of the 66 MPs I've sent to Joey Dis' office, not a single one can be contacted?'

Shampoo: 'Not a single one, Sir. All their mobiles have been switched off.'

Col. Jagee: 'The total and absolute morons. Who asked them to switch their phones off?'

Shampoo: 'You did, Sir. You asked them to remain uncontactable until the job is done.'

Wearing his Saddam Hussein fatigues, complete with a beret, he (Col. Jagee) was tapping his desk with his feet. But that wasn't the peculiar part, the peculiar part was he was standing on it.

Col. Jagee: 'But the job isn't done?'

Shampoo: 'Afraid it is, Sir.'

Col. Jagee: 'If it's done, then they should have contacted me. So it's not done.'

Shampoo: 'Actually it is done, but not in that way Sir.'

Col. Jagee: 'If they have not completed the job, Shampoo, the job is not done. So pray in what way is the job done if the job has not been done?'

Shampoo tried to explain with the same success he'd have had teaching the rudiments of trigonometry to a tarantula spider. Meanwhile the tarantula spider in question was in a highly perplexed state.

Col. Jagee: 'If the rumour is that they are buying our MPs, then tell me pray with what money? Isn't all their money tied up in that birthday celebration in North Korea?'

Shampoo: 'I don't know, Sir, but I think the answer is with Mohan Huskee'.

Col. Jagee: 'Mohan Huskee is missing.'

Shampoo: 'Precisely. I think that's your answer.'

Col. Jagee: 'Betrayed by my own people. Shampoo, you think that nitwit lied...set us up?

Shampoo: 'I think so, Sir.'

Col. Jagee: 'Well, Shampoo, we may be in a corner,

we may be in dire straits, but leadership is defined by moments like this. I know exactly what to do.'

Shampoo: 'What Sir?'

Col. Jagee: 'I need a massage. See if anyone's free please, otherwise it will have to be you.'

Shampoo: 'Sir please, this maybe make or break for the Sandwich Party. You've got to do something.'

Col. Jagee: ' Your right. Sorry, what was I thinking? I'm the President; I need to steer the ship. Got it? I'll run on the treadmill first, then get me that message.'

Shampoo was about to protest, but he was too late. The treadmill had started with Col. Jagee astride it, sans clothes, but proudly wearing his beret.

In the early hours of Wednesday morning, across the length and breadth of Bey, Col. Jagee mounted his last stand. Okay, okay, that sentence came out all wrong, Col. Jagee's cut-outs were mounted on stands and placed all over the city. Placed where they could do the most damage—near schools, in front of hospitals, on top of bridges, on the main road, in the lobby of residential buildings. His supporters roamed the streets with their one-time offer i.e. basically you are offered a chance to support and vote for Col. Jagee's party. This offer is made to you one time only after which the supporters would break your legs. This was a very sensible way to garner support and you will be surprised at the number of people who'd prefer not to have their legs broken, and instead choose to support Col. Jagee. As political ideologies go, avoiding breaking your legs is as good a one as any. It was not an original idea. Stalin and Nicolae Ceausescu used it this century and Caligula and Nero were amongst the earliest and most deadly exponents of this craft. First Bey, and then across GYAANDOSTAAN, this last stand played out. Sadly the one thing Col. Jagee's supporters couldn't do was actually go in the following booth with the citizens and ensure their loyalty. The polling booths were manned by the army. The army was still recovering from the man who made himself a self-styled Colonel. Sandwich Party goons armed with hockey sticks and kitchen appliances were no match for the machine gun-wielding men in fatigues.

We must now leap forward. You and me are together, dear reader. Trusting in each other in an expression of blind faith. Democracy is without doubt two things. First, it is the most boring form of government, futile and apathetic, and second, it is the slowest, the longest, the most-time consuming process since the institution of marriage.

The electoral process is so long in the execution that we have proof today that no one single person on the face of this earth knows the entire process down to the last comma. The one person who apparently did, a certain Theodius B. Clyde of Great Britain, hung himself to death, upside down, just to escape the tedium initiated by the democratic electoral process. So, dear reader, if I get your affirmation—and please feel free to check with the other readers first—we will then skip this process and land our story back forward (yes, a paradox in terms) to the Bigger House of Parliament in Bey, GYAANDOSTAAN.

It is the day after the elections, noon. The Parliament is full, the press and many supporters are crammed in. Under GYAANDOSTAAN law (which as you know is based loosely on Alexander the Great's gift to good governance and law titled 'Don't Drink and Diatribe'), the public prosecutor is the man who announces the Grand election results. The man in question in our story, let me remind you, is the man with that tropical fruit in his name, Mr Gomango Bosh.

The Sandwich Party was conspicuous by its largely absent population. It looked like chutney without the bread. Hardly a healthy-looking Sandwich.

Col. Jagee cut a solitary figure. Only Shampoo and two of his legal advisors sat near him. Shampoo had already saved his bacon once that morning, as the Colonel had entered parliament without his pants. An oversight, or undersight, depending on perspective. Be that as it may, he was now well ensconced in a white shawl that belonged to the canteen lady. But what he really had on that day was a scowl. What the canteen lady had on was unmentionable.

The Ball and Socket Party looked like a group of young bulls in season. Bursting and full of energy. Ray Chow had his lucky sequined bush shirt on. The one which had pictures of two white rhinos in the throes of passion.

Mr D'Souza, still disgruntled with his celebrity status in China and nowhere else, had on his lucky cap. Paul Huskee and Colleen Connor sat holding hands with even greater expectation than the rest.

Gomango Bosh: 'It's been a lightening elections. Congrats to the sitting government for putting on such a good show. Even the Beyside School Elementary's election process involves a whole week, so this is the fastest election since Alexander the Great voted for himself in 334 B.C. And now for the results.'

While Gomango paused as a good orator should, Col. Jagee fiddled with his pen. Then, in the universal sign of a person feeling the pressure, he started pulling at the shirt and licking lips. Which would have gone unnoticed if they were his own. Paul Huskee said a little prayer and Gomango continued.

Gomango Bosh: 'Communists: total 1, same as last time; Independents: total 23, down 17 from last time; Ball and Socket Party: 202, which means they have a simple majority and must be invited to form the new government.'

Parliament was on its feet. All were cheering. Sandwich Party members were rushing to switch sides as all good politicians should do in a functioning democracy. Col. Jagee started banging his head on his desk and yelling and yelling, 'Cheaters! Liars! It's all fixed.' A real irony as cheating, lying, and fixing is what he had dedicated his life to. Meanwhile, his legal aides started whispering something to him. Shampoo heard it and was horrified. Col. Jagee got that gleam in his eye. He let the shawl fall to the ground as he rose bare legged and alighted Gomango Bosh's now vacant podium.

Col. Jagee: 'Hear, Hear!!! I declare this election result null and void!!!'

It took a few minutes but the celebrations stopped.

Col. Jagee: 'The Ball and Socket Party is disqualified under Article 17 C, para 4 (II) which states: If the leader of a political party is enjoying an illicit affair not solemnized by marriage, then in the case of his party winning, he and his party are disqualified, and the second placed party may form the government.'

There was a huge silence in the room. It was so quiet that even the pins didn't bother dropping. Everyone looked at Paul Huskee and Colleen O'Connor, the illicit love story.

16

You've all seen the stories. Watched the movies. You know, I'm speaking specifically of the point in them when something remarkable happens. In *King Kong*, it was when Mr Kong realized he loved the girl. In *The Big Boss*, it was when Bruce Lee realized he was in the wrong movie. In this case, that point is now—that melodramatic, irrational, unbelievable moment that changes the situation from an almost hopeless one.

Parliament was in a state of shock. Euphoria was switching drastically downward to disbelief, despair, and finally fear . Ball and Socket MPs were sweating and softly swearing. Independents and Sandwich Party MPs who had sold out took it one step further and started choking themselves. Shampoo was for once at a total loss, having been caught out by this development. Only Col. Jagee leaned his chair back and put his bare feet on the table. An act of a man who was very much in charge. As he gazed at the dazed minions around, he thought of all the wonderful things he'd do to all the traitors and cynics. His clean thoughts included mangled body parts and lots of terrified screaming. He smiled his happy smile, wriggled his toes, threw his head back, and then it happened! The front doors were flung open and a shadowy figure, with a long grey beard, escorted by a veritable platoon of bodyguards entered. There was an audible gasp of surprise, excitement, and relief (though the last one was from those who had been choking themselves relentlessly and needed to take a break). The man walked with his proud posse, right to Paul Huskee's chair. Then, putting a hand on his shoulder in a reassuring manner, he patted him like one would a nervous puppy. He then gradually moved to the podium and began to address the gathering.

'Oh my God!' Col. Jagee looked like he had seen a ghost which was perfectly natural, as he clearly had. 'I'm back,' said a voice from way down below hidden in the longest, thickest beard since man evolved away from sheep. Now the hall was alive and excited. There was a buzz, though later that proved to have come from the vacuuming lady who had begun her shift, oblivious to all.

Jay Huskee: 'I'm Jay Huskee and I've been missing for over a year. My story is sad to tell, a teenage ne'er do well.'

Then realizing he had broken into the lyrics of his favourite song from *Grease (the musical)*, he stopped and started again.

Jay Huskee: 'All I remember is this and that, less this and more that, but I owe GYAANDOSTAAN an explanation. So I thought of one on my drive here from the airport. On that particular night, I was leaning on my balcony window when I heard the sound of a rhinoceros charging a building. This confused me as there was no rhinoceros in GYAANDOSTAAN, and no other building next to ours. I leaned out of the window to see what I could ascertain, and I heard the sound again. Only I could find no rhino on the main street at the time. I leaned further, then sourced out the sound. It was coming from behind me. Right behind me. I screamed in terror and looked behind, and in doing so lost my bearing and with it my balance. As I fell out of the window, one thing became clear. The rhino was actually Mr D'Souza sneezing. As I fell from the balcony, many thoughts clouded my head. Chief amongst them was, *Had I remembered to switch all the lights before leaving*? I also seemed to remember the words to the second verse of the French National Anthem, something I've never able to achieve before. I also remember seeing the look on Mr D'Souza's face, and I did recall thinking to myself that he did look like a rhinoceros. But that still didn't explain the mystery of the building or buildings nearby. As luck would happen, I fell into an open truck filled with seaweed. The seaweed cushioned my fall which is why I would like to dedicate the rest of my life to saving seaweed from extinction which I was told may happen by March 3037 A.D., but definitely by July 16 of the following year. At this point I lost consciousness, not from the fall but as a consequence of the seaweed aroma. (Keep in mind in Pupric or GYAANDOSTAAN, seaweed may be spelt without the hyphen and is pronounced as "Khurshid".) When I woke up, I found myself on a ship bound for Oceania. My only companion at this point was the seaweed. Later on, I was introduced to the Captain. This introduction took all of three days due to the language problem. The Captain of the ship, whose name was Oleg, or possibly Peter, was Russian. The crew was entirely Vietnamese, except for the chief engineer who was from Somalia, but with no criminal record.

'Thus for the first few hours, it was the seaweed which made the most sense. Through trial and error, I found out that the ship's name was Constantine, though later it was changed to Esther Williams behind the Captain's back. Initially I asked for a mobile phone to call home for help. But I couldn't remember any number, so I played Angry Birds till the phone battery died. I also found out that the ship had bought seaweed from GYAANDOSTAAN and was on its way to sell it to companies in Sweden. Since I always wanted to visit Scandinavia and because I had gotten such a warm response from the seaweed, I decide to tag along. Though I did have a disagreement with the Captain who refused to sail to Sweden via Boston despite my repeated pleas that Boston was where my cousins Poo and Py live.

'In Sweden, I really planned to phone home or at least email, but since I couldn't remember numbers, and didn't know how to use a computer, I had to abandon that plan. A Swedish acquaintance suggested homing pigeons. But in the middle of training a dove I called "Clitus", I was arrested for animal cruelty and had to pay a small fine as well as abandon Clitus who I had got quite fond of. But I did learn an important lesson—pigeons don't really fetch balls;

that's best left to retrievers. I then decided (At this point parliament started emptying out.) to approach the GYAANDOSTAANI embassy which was located at the back portion of a Bangladeshi restaurant called "So Calcutta". At the front desk, I met a beautiful Japanese girl called "Yuki". We fell in love and got married 2 months later. I found the language problem to be greatly beneficial. It becomes increasingly difficult to get frustrated with your partner when you don't know what he or she is saying. Initially everything went well though slowly I did start missing the seaweed which seemed to have left their indelible mark on my heart, as well as perhaps smell. (At this point 80 percent of parliament had left.) I looked for jobs in Sweden and found three—two I returned. The third one, "Cake Shop Window Dresser", really caught my fancy. Soon Yuki and I decided to have our own little babies. But there weren't any available. This seemed to frustrate, and one morning she left for Japan after leaving me a note. But since the note didn't say anything, I had no idea why. Then I turned to poetry and both my poems were both translated into Swedish, and immediately, for some inexplicable reason, translated back into GYAANDOSTAANI where I found to my horror one had become one stanza shorter!'

(At this point only the main players and a handful of journalists were left in Parliament.)

Col. Jagee was quite beside himself. His ally and benefactor was rambling on and on.

Col. Jagee: 'Okay, whatever happened Jay, don't forget you are an office bearer of the Sandwich Party.'

Jay Huskee: 'But that's just it. I arrived yesterday, resigned from the Sandwich Party, and became the President, and thus leader, of the Ball and Socket Party. This I did not because of the family connection, but because they assured me they always break for lunch. But we digress; let me return to Sweden, where after my wife left, I embarked on a soul searching mission which included poetry, pottery, and poster making.'

At this point, a furious Col. Jagee interrupted, shouting loudly with his hands above his head.

Col. Jagee: 'Get to the point. Have you resigned? Who are you with? Who are you?'

Jay Huskee: 'When I returned, I contacted my old friend and classmate Gomango Bosh who we used to call BooBoo. BooBoo filled me in on all the goings-on off the last few months. He also mentioned the three-card trick you maybe resorting to, and it was he who advised me to take over the leadership of the party. Since all the papers of both parties are with him, we drew up the fresh clauses late yesterday evening. All this was known only to Ray Chow, BooBoo, and me. We had to include Ray as he paid for my cab fare from the airport, as well as gave me a place to stay for the night. You see I wanted to make a grand entry and supervise everybody. Besides, in GYAANDOSTAAN, as you very well know, all barbers are closed on Tuesday so I couldn't even get a haircut and shave.'

Col. Jagee now screamed, 'That doesn't change the fact that your party is disqualified.' Gomango Bosh now joined his friend at the podium mike.

Gomango Bosh: 'Oh, but it does. Legally at the time of counting, Jay Huskee is the leader of the Ball and Socket Party. Col. Jagee, your reign is over, and after taking the oath, and getting a haircut and shave, Jay Huskee will be announced as the new President of GYAANDOSTAAN.'

The few people left in the building started clapping. Paul Huskee and gang rushed to the elder Huskee and started to throw him up in the air. President Jagee pushed Shampoo aside and started to throw up. He found all his supporters disappearing from the corner of his eye. In true GYAANDOSTAANI tradition, all who were left in the building had aligned themselves with the Ball and Socket Party. It was the end of

President Col. Jagee. Well, that's probably not fair. We can't say for certain beyond this particular book, but for this manuscript, strictly speaking, it was the end of Col. Jagee. We leave him there in the GYAANDOSTAANI Parliament, vomiting and bitter, like a fallen Caesar, only a little fatter and with no holes in his torso. So, where were we? Ah, it was the end of Col. Jagee... er...or was it?

It took some time for the dust to settle. Shampoo, in the meantime, decided to resign from his post. At which point he realized he didn't have any post. So after reaching the safety of the Ball and Socket office, he sent Col. Jagee an e-mail.

Dear Mr Col President Jagee. I can't lie to you anymore. First off, let me tell you that I'm a no. 7 Dan karate belt holder, nor did I invent the sport of Taekwondo. Also, I am not a certified Yoga teacher from Delhi University. I am actually, as certified by the University of Rangoon, a level 3 Yoga teacher. Also, my real name is not Shampoo, although due to security implications I dare not reveal my real, real name. For now, it's sufficient to say it's not Shampoo. Also my sister is not married into the Royal family of Spain. In fact, the truth is my sister isn't married at all. And if we dig a little deeper, in actuality I don't even have a sister. I am a loyal card carrying member (though I have recently misplaced it) of the Ball and Socket Party.

The intention was to get close to you in order to filter information from your camp, and there is no party money in North Korean banks. That was just to lull you into elections. Paul Huskee's brother, by the way, says hi. Having said that, I would want to put down for the record that since you yourself are of a duplicitous nature, you'd be far better placed to appreciate such duplicitous behaviour. I must say on one level I did enjoy my time with you. Though for a Head of State, if you don't mind the criticism, you really need to wear more clothes or at least some clothes or a small cloth at least, maybe?

You also need to get yourself some good advisors. Advisors from your own party. Also these advisors should and must have clothes. I would like to stay in touch, but I'm told you are in a very bad mood. This I've gauged from the fact that you tried to eat your pajamas at the press conference that announced the handover of power. I'm also told that you are a tad disappointed with me. This can be gauged from the fact that you said you want me tied to four horses and pulled in different directions. Let me assure you there is no need for that. I am, I must tell you, an expert horseman quite capable of riding the horses. So please, there is no need to tie me to them in this case. All in all, it's been an enjoyable relationship. Thank you and wish you the best.

P.S: Mr Col. Prez. what would you like me to do with all your naked photographs? I have over 5,000 of them, and there must be some way to put them all to good use?

Yours faithfully

(   )

Shampoo didn't sign off on the email, as he felt, as he usually did, too much information was very harmful to all concerned parties.

The ancient Sumerians have a saying that dates back 3,000 years. 'No critic can a film make'. This also explains why till today no ancient Sumerian has won a BAFTA or even a Golden Globe, let alone an Oscar. A week after the new government was formed, Paul Huskee found himself beset with problems. The new President Jay Huskee had fallen in love with a Latvian model and had made up his mind to follow her to Latvia which would have at least made a little sense if she had heard about him. To make sure the government didn't fall, Mr D'Souza was made head of the Ball and Socket Party, which meant he now became the President of GYAANDOSTAAN. This meant GYAANDOSTAAN had four Presidents in seven days, a world record. The good thing about Mr D'Souza's accession was that he had no idea that he'd been made President and Paul Huskee decided for the sake of stability in government nobody should inform him of the same for at least a year.

How they arrived at D'Souza for President is an interesting story. It all began when Jay Huskee was arrested for repeatedly stalking the Latvian woman. After Gomango, BooBoo, and Bosh had the charges dropped on grounds of insanity (the Latvian woman's),

Paul Huskee realized they needed a more viable option for leader.

And while Jay Huskee was packing his bags for a new life in Latvia, which he erroneously thought included the above mentioned Latvian woman, the Ball and Socket's inner circle sat down to solve the dilemma. And yes, scientifically no Ball and Socket should have an inner circle, no doubt, but in this case they needed to strengthen their hold on GYAANDOSTAAN before Jay Huskee started making Col. Jagee look good.

As Jay Huskee was still around, Paul had all the windows left open, in silent hope. So who should be nominated for President? The candidates and the minions researched long and hard. They argued back and forth. Finally, after all arguments and debates were played out, they decided to go by the Abraham Constitution which states that in such a tight situation the responsibility should go to the person or persons who didn't attend the meeting. So, it was that the newly crowned China superstar Mr D'Souza received the highest position in GYAANDOSTAAN, and just because he was ignorant of the fact still took nothing away from the enormity of the feat. And as the ancient Sumerians are likely to say (though generally in ancient

Sumerian), 'The best leader is he who hasn't yet been informed that he is the leader'. And Mr D'Souza should know because whatever he said simply sounded like ancient Sumerian.

Now Mr D'Souza was not an elected member of Parliament, but according to the GYAANDOSTAANI constitution, as long as he got himself through any by-election within 2 years of assuming office, he could continue his good work at the top.

17

The swearing in ceremony was another thing all together. During Mr Gomango Bosh's opening investiture ceremony, he spoke of and extolled the virtues of Mr D'Souza. Since this was a pure work of fiction, there was laughter all around. It must be said that some were moved to tears. Moved to tears by their unquenchable laughter. Two moments stand out: When Gomango Bosh spoke of Mr D'Souza as the 'most well-read citizen of GYAANDOSTAAN', people were doubling up in mirth. When he described Mr D'Souza as 'China's most popular celebrity', many fell off their chairs laughing. Mr D'Souza, seated on the dias bang in the centre and on the right of Gomango Bosh, was, as usual, fast asleep though the festivities.

The fun really just started when he was woken up and taken to the podium which he promptly cleaned, and then returned to his seat. The second time around he was made to adopt the posture and take oath of office. The posture meant raising of the right leg, right hand, and right eyebrow simultaneously. This tradition dates back to another Alexander the Great moment. Alex was said to have adopted this posture just before his second bath. (Alexander was a notorious non-bather, but found the dusty clime of GYAANDOSTAAN quite unbearable and so insisted on bathing 3 times a day, twice with soap and often in the middle of a pitched battle.) Legend has it, not satisfied by the soap served by a cook of GYAANDOSTAANI descent, he stood with his right foot on the fellow's back and admonished him sternly. It is said that so irritated was Alexander with this person that his right eyebrow was arched hideously high throughout his rant. Legend has it that the right eyebrow never descended long after this incident took place. It may also explain why in Central Asia, boys born with one eyebrow on top of the other are often named Alexander.

Mr D'Souza finally took the oath which read, 'I, Mr D'Souza, as leader of the GYAANDOSTAAN nation, do solemnly pledge to conduct myself with honour, truth, valour, and integrity while leading myself and my people away from temptation and into the security of sovereignty and freedom. This I swear, by God.'

Mr D'Souza's speech should have taken 9 seconds. Try it yourself, dear reader. Read this passage and time yourself. 9 seconds, right?

D'Souza was forced to repeat himself 29 times as no one was sure of what he had said. He initially appeared to talk of cleaning new watering holes for elephants somewhere down the line. It appeared to be more on the lines of South East Asia on a shoestring budget. It seemed to take a turn for the worse, when his oath was about the contribution of earwax to a developing nation's economy. Exasperated and desperate, Paul Huskee produced a medical certificate saying that Mr D'Souza had laryngitis and so requested the house that he take oath on the new President's behalf. The house concurred quickly as Mr D'Souza was now quite unbearable. After the oath was completed, Mr D'Souza was placed on his chair by 4 people. Whilst seated, he continued to assume the position of one leg, one arm, one eye raised. GYAANDOSTAAN had earned a new government under a new leader. No point telling you about Mr D'Souza's first interview as President that ran on the state television. That it took 3 days to complete didn't make the 10 minute interview any more worthwhile to watch.

But as Col. Jagee set in the West of GYAANDOSTAAN,

a new star arose in her East—Mr D'Souza. The new President, of course, had one clear advantage over all his contemporaries. He had no idea he was the President of GYAANDOSTAAN.

It was the famous Russian revolutionary B.L.S.Trotsky who in his famous book *Oh Crap! I've Made a Huge Mistake* said, 'Governing is worse than gardening, and in gardening at best you can talk to your plants.' Paul Huskee and gang soon got down to the business of governance. They found that Col. Jagee had left them a rich legacy, a rich legacy of debt. The Canadian government was owed 100 million Ragoos and with the change in government, as always happens, Canada started asking. The debt continued. 75 million from the World Bank, 90 million from Japan. A pipeline that was in the pipeline for the last 16 years with Azerbaijan, whose investment of close to 60 million could not be returned. Rice from India, IT from China, ball bearings from Switzerland....

The Ball and Socket were suitably impressed. Col. Jagee had buried the country in debt. Strangely, as long as he was in power, the creditors hadn't been calling. But now the phone and emails were flying thick and fast. No one had warned Paul Huskee about the futility of governance. If only he had gotten a chance to speak to Trotsky!

Let's now sit in on a conversation of the cabinet, inventors of the GYAANDOSTAANIS' insurmountable debt. The coterie sat around Paul Huskee's oak table in the old Ball and Socket office. They had refused to move into Col. Jagee's old office—the official Presidential workplace. This was for two good reasons. Firstly, it was quite a distance away and secondly, Col. Jagee still occupied it and wasn't planning on leaving any time soon. Bella Terrace seemed the most agitated. While all eyes were on Amama, the planner, the visionary, it was Ray Chow who did all the talking.

Ray Chow: 'We could run.'

Bella Terrace: 'Run?'

Ray Chow: 'Yes, we could abandon ship and just run. They love Mr D'Souza in China. We could all move there, lock, stock, and two smoking barrels (keep in mind this phrase was used by Ray Chow well before a British filmmaker made a popular film with the same title). The situation is helpless anyway, we can't stem the debt.'

Shabbir Hoosein: 'I agree. I still can't give you a

cumulative number, but the debts are unanswerable. As a country, we don't exist. So yes, Ray's right, except I think we should go to South Africa and settle there.'

Paul Huskee: 'Why South Africa?'

Shabbir Hoosien: 'Well for one thing, I haven't been there yet.'

Bella Terrace: 'What about India?'

Shabbir Hoosien: 'Oh God, no! India? Have you seen their films?'

Ray Chow: 'China is the only alternative. We have huge leverage, thanks to Mr D'Souza.'

Ray Chow left the room to attend a call, almost relieved by the event. Colleen Connor was the voice of reason. She screamed. This seemed to quieten the chaos.

Colleen Connor: 'It's not so difficult. We just had to do what every government, every monarch, every statesman worth his salt has done from time immemorial. We are no different from the early Ottoman empire or the Anglo-Saxons under Alfred the Great.'

Paul Huskee had become a patient man and politics had made him even more patient. But he stretched his brow in such a quizzical expression that it was made abundantly clear he had run out of epidemics.

Colleen Connor: 'All we need to do is stall, buy time. You know, come up with a typical 5-year plan. Haven't you all understood anything about stalling both public and payments until the next government inherits the headache? We just need to do a holding job.'

Paul Huskee: 'Okay, holding job is fine, but these guys all had their deals with the devil. And the devil is no longer President. So naturally they want us to honour their contracts. They're hungry and insecure, so how the hell do we stall them?'

At this point Ray Chow entered the room. From his broad smile they knew he had the answer. The smile and the fact that he was pulling on Shabbir Hoosein's nose with great glee.

Now, dear reader, it's time to close the story. Weave a silken thread that brings the tale to its end. Since that would require a skilled professional let's do the next best thing—let's examine the contracts.

The contracts with China hold the key to GYAANDOSTAAN's future. I would share them with you, but both you and I know this would be a pointless exercise as they are written in Chinese and

GYAANDOSTAANI. When Ray Chow answered the call from China, he was reminded by the lawyers from the other side (they could be from China but are lawyers truly 'from' anywhere?) that some of the finer points of the contract had still to be honoured. Since Ray Chow, Amama, Mr D'Souza, and the rest of the Ball and Socket gang had, in true political style, no clue of what exactly was in the contracts, he asked sheepishly for a quick reminder. I won't bother you, dear reader, with a lot of details, as I know you need to read another book quickly to get this book out of your system, but here are the bullet points:

1. For the next 5 years, GYAANDOSTAAN is listed as a public limited company and listed on the New York Stock Exchange.
2. 51 percent equity is owned by China and 49 percent by the Ball and Socket Party. Thus, effectively for the next 5 years, China will own GYAANDOSTAAN.
3. China will now inherit GYAANDOSTAAN's national debt which they will clear happily.
4. In return, all road signs will be in Chinese. Chilly chicken, chowmein, and American chopsuey will be wiped out of GYAANDOSTAAN, eradicated completely, as they are not, and never have been,

a part of Chinese cuisine. Anyone found making or eating them will be shot.

5. All road signs will be alternately named after Sun-Yat-Sen or Chairman Mao.
6. GYAANDOSTAAN will be renamed Sino GYAANDOSTAAN.
7. Anyone not using the official name would be kept in an ice-box indefinitely.
8. Ice-boxes to be made in Sino GYAANDOSTAAN, not China.
9. Badminton to be made compulsory.

Then there were particulars about how China's will must prevail in corporate governance, defense, and law and order. Also mundane smaller facts like ethnic GYAANDOSTAANIS should walk on the left side of the road, they mustn't have homes above the third floor, and spitting is only allowed if done on one's own shoes.

The Ball and Socket Party accepted these proposals especially the ones that haven't been mentioned quite happily. Well, actually, they had accepted these terms and conditions long ago when they signed the contracts in China without reading any of them which is always the only successful way to deal with a contract in the first place.

Paul Huskee and his team soon became world

celebrities, being the first country in the world to be wholly sponsored by another country. Thus, Sino GYAANDOSTAAN became the World Brand Ambassador for China. And if by this move it did nothing else but remove chilli chicken from our collective palates, then it had not to be seen as a mundane, but a positive and progressive move.

However, for GYAANDOSTAAN, sorry Sino GYAANDOSTAAN (not a big fan of living in an ice bucket), was this the end, the beginning of the end, the end of the beginning, or just the middle? Only time would tell. Time which would now be read in Chinese.

Epilogue

Paul Huskee, Jay Huskee, Col. Jagee , Mr D'Souza, Ray Chow, Amama, Bella Terrace, Mr Connor... It's been a long journey and now, dear reader, those who have been loyal must be rewarded. It is important to never leave a tale half-complete. Homer did that with the *Illiad* with disastrous consequences. Here quarter complete yes, but half complete never. As a school boy I spent sleepless nights wondering what happened to Achillies' other heel? If Helen ever had children out of wedlock? And whether the usually challenged Homer was ever able to check his own spellings!

So what of Gyaandostaan? What happens to our group of intrepid and not-so-intrepid characters? Let's look twenty years on. Now obviously to find out where everything stood, I needed to speak to a clairvoyant. But my problem with clairvoyants since my childhood seems incurable. They are just too expensive. So I spoke to my numero who, in a noble misguided effort to get rid of me from his office as soon as possible, helped me come up with the following scenario.

The following is known as 'Twenty Years After' and although inspired by Alexander Dumas, it has actually nothing to do with *The Three Musketeers* or *D'artagnan*.

The country of Gyaandostaan had benefitted greatly by the Chinese takeover. Manufacturing had gone through the roof. And though the bust of Alexander the Great had rather Chinese features, which made him indistinguishable from Chengiz Khan, the relationship between the GYAANDOSTAANI and the Chinese was a harmonious one.

There was a never-seen-before dynamism in the country. A new generation of entrepreneurs. From coffee to charcoal, textiles to IT, they were galloping along. The newly-discovered paper industry displaced Finland's status in the same. Coffee productions challenged Brazil. And when it came to terra-cotton fishing nets which kept the fish warm single-handedly revived the fishing sector worldwide.

Paul Huskee and Colleen O'Connor got married and of course went on a children spree. But after adopting 5, they were quite disgruntled and switched to Doberman Pinschers.

Amama became the Finance Minister of Gyaandorstaan and then went on to serve as Ambassador to Japan where he became the only adult made to never pass the yellow belt exam in Karate despite 33 effort laden attempts.

Ray Chow whose team invented the terra-cotton fishing nets became the richest man in GYAANDOSTAAN and was in the *Forbes* richest list for 27 consecutive years. And surprise, surprise—his second in command was Gulu.

Bella Terrace finally married Mr D'Souza although Mr D'Souza didn't actually propose. But phonetically there really is very little to choose from. Will you hurry please and will you marry me.

Mr D'souza found himself living with Bella Terrace and spending months at a time in Beijing where he was now China's greatest living icon ever. By now he'd given up trying to figure out why things were happening as they did. The SWIM brothers had joined an Ashram in nearby India, but only after winning 9 reality TV shows in the same country.

Jay Huskee had joined a peace-keeping force in West Africa but fell out of a moving jeep on the Rwanda border and was not seen since.

Col. Jagee revised the genre of 'B' grade Martial Art films. He earned quite a name for himself, and his film *Nonstop Kung Fu* in which all he wore was a nan chaku was voted worst film ever by a group of a hundred of the world's most well-known film critics.

As for you, dear reader, I'm not sure what happens to you twenty years later. But I know this book has aged you as it has aged me.

Please spread the tale of Gyaandostaan—a country small in status but great in spirit and mind. A tale told by an idiot signifying nothing.

Acknowledgements

I'd like to thank my parents, all seven of them, two of whom I'm slightly more attached to. I'd also like to thank the women that inspire me, namely my cleaning lady Sushila, who ensures I raise my feet from the ground every morning for four minutes while she mistakenly cleans the floor. I'd like to thank you, and the man seated on your right. But most of all I'd like to thank the traffic in South Mumbai which has allowed me plenty of time to write.

A Note on the Author

Firstly, the author, who used to be a woman, prefers the term 'lady', though he'd kill for 'Dame' and would rather be killed before he endorses 'broad'. The author has written 437½ books, unfortunately 2 of which have been published. His last work on the electrical dynamic that is the pre-natal child care world, was incredibly rejected by this same publisher. This makes what Queen Elizabeth did to Sir Walter Raleigh into a far smaller crime. The author hates biking, riding, reading, movies, and walks on the beach. He loves working with multiple NGOs, none of whose full forms he cares to remember. His last two experiments with hygiene and fashion failed miserably. So for the sake of his two young children, Mikhaail and Maya, let's hope this books works.